P9-CFV-417

Julius Lester, author of *To Be a Slave*, the 1968 Newbery Medal runner-up, is a man of many parts: columnist, folk singer, radio personality, and photographer. He has written *Look Out, Whitey! Black Power's Gon' Get Your Mama!*, *Search for the New Land*, and *Revolutionary Notes*. His writings have appeared in *The Guardian*, *Broadsides*, *Liberation*, and *Sing Out*. On WBAI, the Pacifica Foundation station in New York, his program has served as a forum for black viewpoints. He has also cut two albums for Vanguard Records.

Tom Feelings has illustrated many books with distinction, none more so than *To Be a Slave*. His own book, *A Black Artist's Pilgrimage*, is a book of people he has drawn and known in New York's ghettos, in the American South, and in West Africa.

Julius Lester

Black Folktales

Illustrated by Tom Feelings

GROVE PRESS, INC., NEW YORK

Other Books by Julius Lester

LOOK OUT, WHITEY! BLACK POWER'S
GON' GET YOUR MAMA!
REVOLUTIONARY NOTES
TO BE A SLAVE

Text copyright © 1969 by Julius Lester
Illustrations copyright © 1969 by Tom Feelings
All Rights Reserved

No part of this book may be reproduced,
for any reason, by any means, including any
method of photographic reproduction,
without the permisssion of the publisher.

This edition published by arrangement
with the Richard W. Baron Publishing Co.

ISBN: 0-394-17178-0
Grove Press ISBN: 0-8021-4067-x

Library of Congress Catalog
Card Number: 73-89956

First Black Cat Edition 1970

14   13   12   11   10

Manufactured in the United States of America
DISTRIBUTED BY RANDOM HOUSE, INC., NEW YORK

GROVE PRESS, INC., 196 West Houston Street,
New York, New York 10014

*In memory of
Zora Neale Hurston,
who made me
glad I am me,
and to
H. Rap Brown*

Foreword

Folktales are stories that give people a way of communicating with each other about each other—their fears, their hopes, their dreams, their fantasies, giving their explanations of why the world is the way it is. It is in stories like these that a child learns who his parents are and who he will become.

The stories in this book are told in the cities and villages of Africa and on the street corners, stoops, porches, in bars, barber shops, and wherever else in

America black people gather. When somebody says, "Man, you remind me of the time when . . ." everybody knows, here comes a story.

There are many kinds of stories. Stories that partly happened and are partly imagined (but what you imagine can be as real and true as what happens in front of your eyes). There are stories that make you laugh; stories that make you think; stories that make you feel good inside; stories that teach you how to get along in the world; stories that take your mind off your troubles.

Each person who tells a story molds the story to his tongue and to his mouth, and each listener molds the story to his ear. Thus, the same story, told over and over, is never quite the same. But when stories are written in books, people think that this is the only way the story should be and that it cannot be changed. And that is the way a story as a living, growing, changing thing dies. Stories can be changed and should be, as the story teller feels. The stories don't live otherwise.

The stories in this book come from the black people of Africa and Afro-America. Most of them have been written down before, in different words and for different times. Some are still told in Africa, like "The Girl With the Large Eyes" and "The Son of Kim-Ana-u-eze and the Daughter of the Sun and the Moon." Some come from slavery time, like "High John the Conqueror" and "People Who Could Fly."

Some have been told in the South so long that no-body knows where they came from, like "How God Made the Butterflies" and "How the Snake Got His Rattles." Still others, like "Stagolee," belong most to black people in the cities. Not all the stories here started as stories. "Stagolee," for instance, was a song about a man who really lived, and "High John" was three stories, not one. I told about half of these stories first for a book printed in a small edition in 1967 by the Student Nonviolent Coordinating Committee. Black children in various places around the country have made some of them into plays.

These stories are told here not as they were told a hundred years ago, but as I tell them now. And I tell them now only because they have meaning now.

JULIUS LESTER

June, 1969
New York City

Contents

Origins

How God
Made the Butterflies

Well, the Lord had just finished making the world, and he sat back in his big ol' rocking chair to look it over.

"Not a bad job, if I say so myself." He lit up a cigar and was feeling pretty good about it until he noticed that the world looked kind of bare. Fact of the matter was, there wasn't a thing to the world except land, trees, and a whole lot of water. There was even more water than land.

"Wonder how that happened," the Lord wondered. "Seems to me I'd planned for there to be more land than water. Well . . ." He shrugged his shoulders and turned his mind to figuring out how to make the world look a little prettier.

"Give me my pruning shears!" he called out, and one of the little angels ran and got them. Then the great Lord Almighty leaned out of his rocking chair, trimmed the trees, and threw the trimmings all over the empty ground. That made the grass, the bushes, and all the flowers.

"Now that don't look too bad," he said and leaned back again. "Yessir. I've made a mighty pretty world." And so saying, he went to bed to rest up from all the work he'd done. Making a world ain't no easy thing. Takes a whole lot of thinking to make everything fit in place, particularly if it's something that's never been thought of before. So the Lord went on to sleep, looking forward to getting up the next morning and admiring his world some more.

The next morning, the Lord hardly had one eye open before he heard the flowers whispering among themselves.

"It's lone down here," said one flower. "We were put here to keep the ground company and make everything look pretty, but it sure is mighty lonely."

The Lord shook his head in disgust. "Have mercy! You get through making one thing, and the next thing you know you got to make something else to go with it. Gimme them little shears, one of you angels."

An angel brought the Lord the teenichy pair of shears, and he bent over to the earth and started snipping little pieces off of everything—the sky, the ground, the trees, the animals, the bushes, the flowers. Everything and anything he laid his shears on got snipped. The very *idea* of getting complaints about the world, and it wasn't even a day old. *That* was gratitude, and the Lord had a feeling he was going to be getting complaints about the world from now on. He was so mad he didn't care what he snipped, and he snipped all morning long—snip! snip! snip! And then he went back to bed, because he didn't want to hear any complaining about all the snipping he'd done. He had a good mind to just stay in bed forever and let the world handle its own complaints.

Well, when the people looked up and saw these tiny scraps fluttering around, they called them flutter-bys. There were yellow flutter-bys. Those were the ones that had been snipped off the sun. And there were blue flutter-bys. They had been snipped off the sky. And there were white flutter-bys. They'd been snipped off the stars. Every color flutter-by you could think of was fluttering around. There were flutter-bys fluttering around that people didn't even have names for to describe their color.

These flutter-bys got over to our part of the world and, well, you know how it is with us. We always got to have *our* way of saying something. The brother in black is going to say the thing his way or die trying. So when we looked up and saw these things come floating by, we heard some white folks call 'em "flutter-bys," and we fell out laughing. Flutter-bys! White folks put their tongues through all kinds of contortions trying to talk. Flutter-bys! Now who could say that? So we turned that thing around and called them butterflies. That sounded a whole lot better. It was easy on the tongue and easy on the ear, and that's what words were supposed to be.

But white folks are something else. They never will let us have nothing of our own. Uh-uh. If they think we having more fun at something than they are, before God get the news, here they come wanting to get in on it. And not only that, you share it with 'em and before the sun go down that night, they going around talking about it's theirs. So white folks started calling them butterflies, too, and went and stuck it in their dictionary wanting people to believe that they'd had enough sense to think of a word that pretty.

Anyway, that's how the Lord made butter-flies, and why you always see butterflies flying around flowers. They were made to keep the flowers company.

Why Apes Look Like People

For a long time after the Lord created the world, the only creatures on it were the animals. They swam the rivers, climbed the mountains, flew through the air, and lived their lives. They learned who to fear and who to greet as a friend, and they followed the fortunes and misfortunes of the seasons and the years, each day flowing from the one previous and toward the one to come.

One day, the Deer family was drinking at

the lake at that time of the day when the sun seems to stop at the top of the sky. Suddenly, a loud noise caused the air to tremble, and the youngest Deer fell at the water's edge, a trickle of blood coming from its side. Frightened, the other Deer ran to the safety of the woods, except for the oldest child. He, too, was frightened, but his curiosity was so strong that he returned to the edge of the forest, and there hid behind a tree to see if the loud noise was going to be repeated or if anything else were going to happen.

He had scarcely hidden himself when an animal he had never seen came down to the lakeside. It was a horrible-looking creature. It walked on two legs and had no hair except for a little on its small, round head. The Deer had never heard of such an animal. He couldn't even remember his cousin, the Moose, ever talking about such an animal and the Moose would surely have seen such a creature, for he often went up into the high mountains and had seen many strange things.

The creature carried a long piece of wood in one of its paws. It stooped down, lay the piece of wood to one side, and magically began taking the skin off his younger brother with something it clutched in its paw. The Deer's fright became stronger than his curiosity, and he turned and bolted through the forest to tell his father what he had seen.

The father found it hard to believe what his oldest son told him. He had lived a long time, had talked to many animals, and had been many places. He had never heard of any creature such as this.

The next day, however, the father repeated the story to every animal he met. None of them had heard of such an animal, either. Several weeks passed. The Deer family found a new lake to drink from, and they had almost put the incident out of their minds, when, late one afternoon, while resting in a grove of shady trees, the father over-heard two birds talking.

"Did you hear what happened this morning?"

"You mean about the Robin family?" the second bird responded.

"Yes."

"Everybody's been talking about it. One of the Robins was flying home after spending the morning with a sick relative, I heard. Suddenly there was a loud noise, and he fell out of the sky like a dead limb dropping from a tree."

"That's exactly what I heard," the first bird said. "What do you think happened?"

"Well, it sounds to me like he had a sudden attack of some sort. You know, this time of year you have to be careful just what kind of worms you eat. He could've eaten some bad worms, and that could've caused a sudden attack of some kind."

"Maybe so, but I've never heard of anything like that happening before."

"Well, that's true."

"And I heard that after the loud noise, he started bleeding."

"Bleeding!"

The father Deer could contain himself no longer, and he excitedly told the birds what had happened to his youngest child. He described the strange animal his oldest son had seen, but the birds could give him no clue as to what it might be. They promised, however, to keep a sharp eye out for such a creature. They covered many miles in the course of a day and saw many things. In fact, they told him that they would give the description to all the other birds and, without a doubt, if such a creature really existed, one of the birds would see him sooner or later.

Hardly a day had passed when the Hawk happened to see just such an animal near the lake where the young Deer had been killed. The Hawk wanted to get a closer look at the creature, and, although the Hawk knew what had happened to the young Deer and the bird, the Hawk knows no fear. So he folded back his wings and dropped from the sky into a tall tree from which he could observe the new animal.

He watched the animal most of the day and saw it take wood and create a fire. This creature could do what the lightning could do when it struck a tree during a storm. The creature then took a large piece of meat and placed it on the wood, which was turning black. After the meat had turned black, the creature took it out of the fire and began eating it. The Hawk had seen enough, and, spreading his great wings, he went to tell others what he had seen.

By this time, other animals in other parts of the forest had begun to tell stories about a creature who walked on two legs and had no hair, and when the news brought by the Hawk began to spread, no one doubted any longer that a new animal was living among them.

For many days, the animals talked among themselves, wondering what kind of animal it was that talked to no other animal and considered all animals its enemy. Finally, the Rabbit sent word through the forest that all the animals should send a representative to a meeting to discuss the situation. The other animals agreed that the Rabbit always did have good ideas, and the next evening, as the sun was setting, a group of them met in the deepest part of the forest.

"Well, I think everybody knows why we're here," the Rabbit began. "Anybody have any ideas?"

There was a long silence. Finally, the Frog spoke. "Well, Mr. Rabbit, we never had a problem like this."

"That's right," the Elephant added. "This new animal don't obey no rules. There doesn't seem to be anybody he likes."

The other animals muttered in agreement, but no one had any suggestions. They thought for a long while. "Mr. Rabbit?" the Snake asked. "You're a better talker than the rest of us. Maybe if you went and talked to him and explained to him how things are, you know, maybe he'd change his ways."

"That's not a bad idea," the Mouse added.

"He *is* new around here," the Fish commented. "He probably just doesn't know any better."

All the animals thought it was a good idea, so early the next morning the Rabbit went down to the lake to talk to the new animal and explain to him all the rules and regulations they'd worked out for living with one another. Unknown to the Rabbit, the Hawk, high in the sky, had decided to follow him. The Hawk didn't like the Rabbit, but he still didn't like the idea of the Rabbit going to meet the new animal alone. He thought all of the animals had to protect each other until they learned who and what this new animal was. After that, they could go back to doing as they pleased.

The Rabbit hadn't been at the lake for more than a few minutes when he saw the new animal. He hopped over to him, and, before he could get a word out of his mouth, the creature snatched him up into its arms. The Rabbit tried to squirm away, but the creature squeezed him tighter.

With his keen eyes, the Hawk saw everything, and he fell, like a bolt of lightning, to the earth. As he neared the strange creature, he gave a loud shriek, stretched his legs, bared his talons, and dug them into the creature's shoulders. The creature screamed and dropped the Rabbit. The Hawk picked the Rabbit up quickly, remembering not to dig his talons too deeply into the Rabbit's body, and was back into the upper reaches of the sky before the creature's screams had died.

That night, the animals held another meeting at which the Rabbit and the Hawk reported what had happened. The animals quickly concluded that they couldn't risk sending anyone else to hold a conference with the new animal.

"So what do we do now?" the Deer asked.

"Kill him!" the Rabbit exclaimed. "Mr. Lion? You're always roaring like you're the baddest thing around. You go get him."

The Lion shook his head. "One of my cousins tried to fight him, and the creature has a stick that spits fire and kills. That's how my cousin was killed. Seems to me that Mr. Hawk did a pretty good job of saving your life today."

"Yeah, Mr. Hawk. What about you?" the other animals asked all at once. "You can do it."

The Hawk thought it over for a while. He didn't like the idea. He much preferred soaring in the upper reaches of the air away from everyone. He really didn't like being around other animals or even being too close to the ground. In fact, if he could've had his way, there would've been food in the air for him to eat so that the only part of the earth he'd ever have to touch would be the top of a mountain. Once or twice a week he was able to snatch a bird out of the air, but too often he had to come right down to the ground to get food, and he didn't like it too much. So he declined. He'd done all he was going to do. Somebody else had to do something now.

The other animals were angry, but the Hawk wouldn't change his mind. The animals continued to argue with him, and, after a few minutes, he simply spread his wings and, sending a cool breeze over them, he flew back to where the clouds lived.

The animals spent a good hour cussing the Hawk before they calmed down enough to continue with the meeting. After several hours, they decided that part of their problem was that they didn't know what kind of animal it was. If they knew that, it might give them some idea what to do. So they decided that the next morning the Rabbit, the Deer, and the Frog would go up to Heaven to see God. If anybody knew, God had to know.

It was late morning when they got to Heaven, but God was just waking up, and he couldn't see them until he had finished his coffee. The Lord gets kind of grouchy if he doesn't have a cup of coffee in the morning, so they sat on the porch and waited.

Finally, the Lord came out. "Well, well, well," he said, sitting down in his rocking chair. "It's been a long time since any of you have been up here. Must be something wrong." He chuckled.

"I think the last time you brought a delegation up here, Mr. Rabbit, was when you got that petition together asking me to stop wintertime."

The Rabbit smiled sheepishly. "Well, I've gotten used to that, Lord."

"Didn't I tell you you would? I hope everything's all right now."

"Well, Lord, to tell you the truth, everything's not all right."

"What's the matter? You got plenty of water, don't you?"

"Water's fine, Lord, but—"

"Plenty tree-leaves to munch on for snacks?"

"Plenty tree-leaves, Lord. The thing is—"

"Ain't there enough oxygen in the air? I'll have to admit that it took me a while to find just the right amount of oxygen to put in the air, but it's O.K. now, ain't it?"

"Couldn't be better, Lord, but—"

"And I shortened the nights like you asked me to. I just can't see what's wrong this time, Mr. Rabbit."

"Well, Lord, if you'd hush up, I'd tell you!"

"Now just slow down a minute, Mr. Rabbit. I'm just trying to see if my world is functioning all right. First world I ever made, you know, and it wasn't no easy job."

"We understand that, Lord," the Deer said.

"Yes, Lord. We understand that," the Rabbit repeated. "And we think you did a fine job, considering how you're an amateur and all that. However, there's a new animal down there."

"Oh! You must mean Man!" the Lord interrupted.

"Man?"

"Uh-huh. An animal that walks on two legs."

"And ain't got no hair?" the Deer wanted to know.

"That's him," the Lord said. "And let me tell you, it was a hard job putting him together. I remember I started early one Monday morning. I'd had the idea tucked away in my head for a long time, so I figured it wouldn't take me more than a few hours to put him together. Well, let me tell you, Mr. Rabbit—"

"Uh, Lord. We understand. We'd like to hear about it, but we just don't have the time today, Lord. While we're up here talking with you, that man-animal is down there killing everything he can get his hands on."

"What was that?"

"That's the truth, Lord. Now you know how we got things worked out among ourselves, so that the deer know to stay away from the lions, and the ground hog looks out for the snake and the fish try to stay out of the bear's way. It's a pretty good arrangement. We don't have to walk around being afraid of everybody else. But this man-animal!" And the Rabbit, the Deer, and the Frog took turns telling God the entire story.

After they finished, the Lord didn't say anything for a long while. He stared off into space and looked very sad. "Well," he said finally, "I think everything will work out all right. I thought man might have a little trouble getting adjusted to everything, but you take my word for it, everything'll be O.K."

The Rabbit, the Deer, and the Frog expressed some doubts, but after God reassured them several times, they went back and reported to the other animals. Things didn't get better, though. More and more of the man-animals began to appear in the forest, and one evening the birds came home to find that some trees had been cut down, including the one they lived in. Soon the man-animals had cleared a lot of the forest, and the animals moved to another forest. It wasn't long, though, before the man-animals came to that forest and cut it down, and the animals had to move again.

Everywhere the animals lived, the man-animals came. They put airplanes in the air, and the Hawk was sorry that he had not tried to kill the man-animal when he had the chance. They put boats on the water and submarines in the sea. They built roads through the middle of mountains and laid pipes deep in the ground, and the ground hogs and all their relatives had to move. They built cities beside rivers and poured gallons of foul liquids into the rivers, and many fish died. The smoke from their cities filled the air, and no birds could live in the cities. They sprayed plants with liquids, and many animals died because there were no clean plants to eat.

The animals moved to new forests, but the man-animal was never far behind. Finally, the animals were tired of moving. Once again, the Rabbit called a meeting and all the animals came, even the Hawk.

They talked about it for several days. The Bear suggested that they make war on the man-animals, but, after much discussion, they couldn't figure how they could get guns and tanks and airplanes. Eventually, the Owl, who was the wisest of the animals, said, "The only sensible thing we can do is to become man-animals ourselves. That is the only way we will ever be as powerful as they are."

"You're right!" the Rabbit exclaimed instantly.

The other animals agreed, and they quickly formed a delegation to go tell God the news.

When they got to Heaven the next morning, the Lord had already finished his morning coffee and was sitting on the porch reading the paper. "Well," he said, putting the paper down. "How y'all doing?"

"Lord, you got to turn us into man-animals," the Rabbit said immediately. He didn't have time for a whole lot of chit-chat that morning.

"Do what?"

"That's right, Lord. That's the only way we can be as powerful as man-animal is and protect ourselves. Otherwise, we don't stand a chance."

The Lord thought it over for a long while. He didn't want to do it, but things hadn't worked out with man-animal as well as he had hoped. In fact, things had turned out pretty bad. Something should've told him that it was going to turn out that way because he'd had such problems making man-animal. Well, win a few and lose a few, thought the Lord. "O.K., animals. Tomorrow morning there'll be a big pot of oil in the middle of the forest. Every animal who washes himself in that oil will become a man-animal."

The animals cheered and rushed back to tell the others. And when they heard the news, they were delirious with joy.

"When I get to be a man-animal," said the Bear, "I'm gon' get me a car. A red convertible with white seats. Tell me I ain't gon' be tough!"

"Wait'll you see me in one of them continental suits!" the Rabbit exclaimed. "Won't be nobody as dap as me nowhere. All them women gon' look at me and say, 'Who is that fine young daddy?' "

All night long the animals stayed up talking about what they were going to do when they became people. Some had already decided that they were going to form a company to buy land, because if anybody knew what land had oil and gold and silver and everything else on it, they sure did. The Jaguar was already campaigning among the other animals to vote for him for President.

They were making so much noise that the Lord couldn't help but hear them. He listened for a while and became very sad. He couldn't help but think that if they were acting this way now, he didnt want to imagine how they would act when they became people. And the world was in bad enough shape as it was. He was so depressed about it that he was thinking of going off and building

another world. And as he listened to the animals talk about what they were going to do when they became people, he decided that the last thing the world needed was any more people.

So he threw a thunderbolt down from Heaven and broke the pot of oil, and when the animals came upon it the next morning, there were just a few drops left in some of the cracked pieces, and while the other animals were looking at it in shock and amazement, the Ape, the Gorilla, the Chimpanzee, and the Monkey rushed over and washed their faces, hands, and feet in the few drops that remained. And that's why those animals look like people.

Why Men Have to Work

The sky used to be very close to the ground. In fact, it wasn't any higher than a man's arm when he raised it above his head. Whenever anybody got hungry, all he had to do was to reach up and break off a piece of the sky and eat it. That way, no one ever had to work.

Well, it was a fine arrangement for a while, but sometimes people would break off more than they could eat, and what they couldn't eat they just threw on the ground. After all, the sky was so big there would always be enough for everybody to eat. What did it matter if they broke off more than they actually wanted?

Maybe it didn't matter to them, but it mattered to the sky. In fact, it made the sky angry to see itself lying on the ground, half-eaten, like garbage. So one day the sky spoke out and said, "Now look-a-here! Can't have this! Uh-uh. Can't have you people just breaking off a piece of me every time your stomach growls and then taking a little bite and throwing the rest away. Now if y'all don't cut it out, I'm going to move so far away no one will ever touch me again. You understand?"

Well, people got the message. In fact, they were pretty scared, and for a while they made sure that no one ever broke off more of the sky than he could eat. But slowly they began to forget. One day, a man came by and broke off a chunk big enough to feed forty people for a month. He took a few little bites, licked around the edges, threw the rest over his shoulder, and walked on down the road just as happy and dumb as anything you've ever seen. Well, the sky didn't say a word, but with a great roar, the sky lifted itself up as high as it could, and that was pretty high.

When the people realized what was happening, they began crying and pleading with the sky to come back. They promised that they would never do it again, but the sky acted like it didn't hear a word.

The next day, the people didn't have a thing to eat, and they had to go to work to feed themselves, and that's why man is working to this very day.

How the
Snake Got His Rattles

When the Lord made the Snake, he made him all the pretty colors he could think of—reds and browns and oranges—and the Lord put the Snake down here to decorate the ground and the bushes, to add a little color to everything.

Well, the Snake didn't mind ornamenting the earth, but he wondered if the Lord knew what a hard life he had to lead. And it was hard! Wasn't no doubt about that. He didn't have wings like the birds, so he couldn't fly. He didn't have fins, so he couldn't go for a swim in the river. He didn't have feet, so he couldn't run fast. All he could do was crawl in the dust. He didn't even mind that so much, but he couldn't figure out why the Lord had given him such poor eyesight. Man, the Snake was so blind he couldn't even see a flashlight if it was shining right in his eyes. He was so blind he couldn't see his hands in front of his face if he had had hands to put in front of his face. His eyesight was so bad he had to smell his way around. And to tell the truth, his nose was none too good, either.

Now you can imagine what it must've been like when the Snake had to go to the store or down to the laundromat. Crawling around in the dust like that and being half-blind, he was always getting stepped on. He couldn't see anybody coming, and, since he was down on the ground, nobody could see him. The other animals didn't mean to step on him, but you know how it is sometimes. You're in a hurry trying to get somewhere, and you just ain't got the time to see whether there's a blind snake with a no-smelling nose in your path. Some days, the mere thought of going somewhere tired the Snake out so much that he just didn't even bother getting up.

Mrs. Snake wasn't too happy about the situation, either. She couldn't even take the little snakes down to the playground anymore. The other children thought they were pretty jump ropes. So she was stuck in the house with the kids all day, and they were about to drive her out of her mind. "Why don't you do something?" she screamed at him one morning. "I went out to hang up the laundry this morning, and I almost got run down by two buffalo, three antelope, and a rabbit. I'm just sick and tired of this, and if you're half a snake at all, you'll do something about it."

Mr. Snake sighed. He'd heard it all so many times before. "Well, just what do you expect me to do? Grow arms? The Lord made us this way and ain't a thing we can do about it."

"Says who? You know as well as I do that God don't know what he's doing half the time. He just sits up there experimenting with this and that, and we were one of the experiments that didn't turn out well. You're going to do something, or I'm going to know the reason why. You're triflin', lazy, and no 'count. My mama told me not to marry you, and I should've listened to her!" And Mrs. Snake proceeded to call him a whole bunch of dirty names. She even jumped on back in his family and started playing the Dozens.

Said his mama was a lizard and his daddy was a fishing worm.

Well, Mr. Snake was trying to figure what number he should play that day, and he couldn't half concentrate with all the yelling his wife was doing, so he decided to crawl off to Heaven and talk it over with the Lord. He figured that the Lord wouldn't be able to do anything, but at least it would shut his wife up if she got the word directly from God.

About two o'clock that afternoon, the Snake got up to Heaven. The Lord was sitting back in his great rocking chair reading *TV Guide.* "Well, what's going on, Mr. Snake?"

"Ain't nothing happening, Lord. Same ol' same ol'. You know."

"Yeah, know what you mean. Pull up a chair. I was just sitting here seeing what was gon' be on television in 1970. Course, that's a long way off, but I figured I'd check it out now, just in case I wanted to take a vacation about then."

The Snake curled up in a chair.

"Care for a cigar, Mr. Snake?"

"Thank you, Lord, but don't believe I do."

"I've been thinking about cutting down myself. Mrs. God tells me I smoke too much. She says it makes my breath smell bad."

"Is that so?"

"That's what she claims, Mr. Snake, and I just can't understand it. I brush after every meal. Well, that's neither here nor there. What's on your mind? You looking mighty well."

"Well, Lord, I ain't *doing* too well."

"You don't say."

"It's the truth. I hate to come up here bothering you and all, knowing how busy you are, but my wife just wouldn't let me rest until I did something."

"Well, why don't you tell me about it?"

"It's like this, Lord. You know my eyes are kinda bad. Seems to run in my family on both sides of the house. And me being low on the ground like I am, I can't tell when folks are coming down the road. As a result, me and my family are always getting stepped on. And Lord, I just ache all over, and you know I got a whole lot of muscles that can ache. The strain has made my nerves so bad that the rain beating on the leaves makes me jumpy."

"You in bad shape, Mr. Snake."

"I done tried Compoz and everything else you can think of for my nerves, Lord, but don't

nothing help. Some days I think about going outside the house and getting stepped on, and I just don't get out of bed."

The Lord lit one of his big cigars and blew smoke rings for a few minutes. "Well, I didn't mean for nothing like that to happen to you." He reached in his pocket and pulled out a small bottle. "Here. This is poison. You put this in your mouth, and give the rest to all your kin folks. This will be for you to use to protect yourself with. Anybody step on you, you can bite 'em and stick a little poison into 'em."

"Thank you, Lord. I sure thank you."

"Don't mention it, Mr. Snake. Glad to help out when I can. If you have any more problems, you just let me know."

The Snake didn't waste a minute getting down the ladder and going home. When he told his wife about the poison, she was so happy she kissed him. He told her that she best be cool and went to bed.

Well, a few days later, the Rabbit sent word through the forest that the animals had to send their union representative to a meeting. All the animals, that is, except the Snake.

"The meeting will now come to order!" the

Rabbit announced. "Hey, Mr. Elephant! Can't you find a seat somewhere and stop blocking the sun? I don't know why the Lord made the dumbest thing in the forest the biggest."

The Elephant sat down.

"You still blocking the sunlight, Mr. Elephant."

"I'm sorry, Mr. Rabbit."

"Well, I understand that it ain't all your fault. You think you can hold your head to one side so a little light can come through? That's good! Now, everybody know why I called this meeting. It's that Snake! We got to do something, and do it quick, before he kills us all off. I've been to thirteen funerals this week, and today's only Tuesday."

"I know what you mean," the Frog put in. "That Snake killed three of my uncles, seven cousins, two aunts, and my brother-in-law. I have to admit, though, that getting rid of my brother-in-law was kind of a blessing."

"Well, blessing or no blessing, that Snake has been a terror ever since the Lord gave him that poison. He's been biting everything that shakes the bush. He can't see, but ain't a thing wrong with his hearing. Why if he just hear any little thing, he's dead on it."

"And he's got the best aim I've ever seen," the Horse added.

"Who you telling?" exclaimed the Rabbit. "I saw a leaf shake on a bush and I guess you know that's one dead leaf now. Snake put all sorts of poison in that leaf."

"Well, what we gon' do about it?" the Fox wanted to know.

"Tell him to move on over or we'll move on over him," said the Panther. "Tell him the next time he lays his forked tongue on anybody, we're going to off him."

"And suppose he lays his forked tongue on somebody and you *don't* off him," said the Rabbit.

"That's right," the Owl put in. "Hustlers don't call showdowns."

The Elephant said, "We could talk to him real nice-like and let him know that we don't mean him no harm, and all we want is our rights. He should be able to understand that."

"Like I said before, how come the Lord made you so big and gave you such a little brain? If your brain was magnified a hundred times, it would fit into the navel of a gnat and rattle around like a BB in a cornflakes box. Understand! He don't have to understand nothing he don't want to, as long as he's got so much power."

They talked and talked and talked and talked

until the Rabbit got so disgusted he just took off for Heaven by himself. They were going to do all that talking and end up saying they should send somebody to talk to the Lord. The Rabbit wondered if he was the only one of the animals that had any sense.

The Lord was reading the newspaper when the Rabbit came up on the porch. "Yeah, Mr. Rabbit. Just between you and me, I ain't gon' be nowhere to be found between 1960 and 1970. And if you take my word, you'll go somewhere and hide yourself. That's going to be a rough ten years. Yes, yes. I ain't answering no prayers during that time. No, indeed!"

"Lord! What're you talking about?"

"You just remember what I said. O.K.?" He folded the newspaper and put it beside his chair. "Now, what's on your mind?"

"It's that Snake!"

"He was just up here a few days ago."

"Don't you think we know it. You gave him some poison, and he's bitten so many animals that a lot of them are packing up and going North. People are scared to let their wives and daughters go out alone at night. That's the truth! Lord, that Snake has bitten three hundred and thirty-seven animals, five oak trees, seventeen palm trees and one stickerbush. Ha! Ha! Ha! You should've seen him bite into that stickerbush. Ha! Ha! Ha! His wife was pulling stickers off his lip for two hours. Served him right, the low-down—"

"I get the point. You go on back and tell Mr. Snake to get himself up here in a hurry."

"Well, it kind of dangerous to get too close to him, Lord."

"You tell the Elephant to yell the message in his general direction. Ain't a thing wrong with Mr. Snake's hearing."

A few hours later, the Snake was curled up in a chair next to the Lord.

"Lord, I sure want to thank you for that poison you gave me a few days ago. I haven't gotten stepped on since."

"That's just what I wanted to talk to you about. What's this I hear about you using that poison for insurance instead of protection?"

"Well, Lord, you know my eyes ain't too good, and I can't see who's my friend and who come to do me harm. So I just bite everybody that come along, and that way I'm always on the safe side. I've been stepped on so much that I just can't take any chances."

"I can understand that, Mr. Snake. But now you just about terrorized everybody."

"I didn't mean to, Lord. I sure didn't intend to do that."

How the Snake Got His Rattles

The Lord reached in his pocket. "Here. You take these rattles and put 'em on your tail. When you hear something, shake your tail. That'll be a warning. If it's your friend, he'll stop and pass the time of day with you. And if it's your enemy, he'll just keep coming, and, after that, it's you and him. You understand?"

"Yes, Lord. I do. And I thank you. It was getting mighty tiresome biting everything that came along. Mighty tiresome."

And that's how the Snake got his rattles. By that time, though, almost everybody was so afraid of him anyway that hardly anyone ever came around to see him. When they did, though, he shook his tail right hard, and it rattled through the forest, letting everybody know: this is Mr. Snake here. You can't step on me now.

Love

The Girl
With the Large Eyes

Many years ago in a village in Africa, there lived a girl with large eyes. She had the most beautiful eyes of any girl in the village, and whenever one of the young men looked at her as she passed through the marketplace, her gaze was almost more than he could bear.

The summer she was to marry, a drought came upon the region. No rain had fallen for months, and the crops died, the earth changed to dust, and the wells and rivers turned to mudholes. The people grew hungry, and when a man's mind can see nothing except his hunger, he cannot think of marriage, not even to such a one as the girl with the large eyes.

She had little time to think of the wedding that would have been had there been no drought. She had little time to daydream of the hours of happiness she would have been sharing with her new husband. Indeed, she had little time at all, for it was her job each day to find water for her family. That was not easy. She spent the morning going up and down the river bank, scooping what little water she could from the mudholes until she had a pitcher full.

One morning, she walked back and forth along the river bank for a long while, but could find no water. Suddenly, a fish surfaced from the mud and said to her, "Give me your pitcher and I will fill it with water."

She was surprised to hear the fish talk, and a little frightened. But she had found no water that morning, so she handed him the pitcher, and he filled it with cold, clear water.

Everyone was surprised when she brought home a pitcher of such clear water, and they wanted to know where she had found it. She

smiled with her large eyes, but she said nothing.

The next day she returned to the same place, called the fish, and again he filled her pitcher with cold, clear water. Each day thereafter she returned, and soon she found herself becoming fond of the fish. His skin was the colors of the rainbow and as smooth as the sky on a clear day. His voice was soft and gentle like the cool, clear water he put in her pitcher. And on the seventh day, she let the fish embrace her, and she became his wife.

Her family was quite happy to get the water each day, but they were still very curious to know from where she was getting it. Each day they asked her many questions, but she only smiled at them with her large eyes and said nothing.

The girl's father was a witch doctor, and he feared that the girl had taken up with evil spirits. One day he changed the girl's brother into a fly and told him to sit in the pitcher and find out from where she was getting the water. When she got to the secret place, the brother listened to the girl and the fish and watched them embrace, and he flew quickly home to tell his father what he had heard and seen. When the parents learned that their daughter had married a fish, they were greatly embarrassed and ashamed. If the young men of the village found out, none of them would ever marry her. And if the village found out, the family would be forced to leave in disgrace.

The next morning, the father ordered the girl to stay at home, and the brother took him to the secret place beside the river. They called to the fish, and, when he came up, they killed him and took him home. They flung the fish at the girl's feet and said, "We have brought your husband to you."

The girl looked at them and then at the fish beside her feet, his skin growing dull and cloudy, his colors fading. And her eyes filled with tears.

She picked up the fish and walked to the river, wondering what was to become of the child she was carrying inside her. If her parents had killed her husband, would they not kill her child when it was born?

She walked for many miles, carrying her husband in her arms, until she came to a place where the waters were flowing. She knew that suffering could only be cured by medicine or patience. If neither of those relieved it, suffering would always yield to death.

Calling her husband's name, she waded into the water until it flowed above her head. But as she died, she gave birth to many children, and they still float on the rivers to this day as water lilies.

The Son of Kim-ana-u-eze and the Daughter of the Sun and the Moon

When the son of Kim-ana-u-eze came to the age to marry, his father came to him and said, "Have you decided whom among the young girls of the village you wish to marry?"

"I will marry none of them, father."

"Then you love a girl of another village?"

"No. I will not marry any girl of this earth."

"Then whom will you marry?"

"I will marry the daughter of the Sun and the Moon."

The Son of Kim-ana-u-eze

The father looked at his son in amazement. "You have always been more of a dreamer than the other children, but this is ridiculous. No one can marry the daughter of the Sun and the Moon."

"But that is whom I want to marry, father."

And the father left him, wondering why it was his misfortune to have fathered such a son.

The son of Kim-ana-u-eze sat down and wrote a letter, asking Lord Sun and Lady Moon for permission to marry their daughter. He gave it to the Deer and asked him to take it to Heaven. "But I cannot go to the sky," said the Deer.

He gave the letter to the Gazelle. "But I cannot go to the sky," was the answer.

He gave the letter to the Hawk. "You are the most magnificent of birds, Hawk. Surely you can fly to the sky."

"I can only go halfway," the Hawk told him. "Further than that is even too far for me."

The son of Kim-ana-u-eze received the same answer from all of the animals he thought could deliver the letter. He was about to give up ever getting his letter to Lord Sun and Lady Moon when the Frog heard of his problem and went to him. He alone of the animals knew that the people of Lord Sun and Lady Moon came to earth each day to get water. "Give me your letter and I will deliver it, son of Kim-ana-u-eze."

Kim-ana-u-eze became angry. "I am in no mood for jokes, Frog. It is mean of you to come and make fun of me."

"I do not make fun of you. Give me the letter. I will deliver it."

"You are a frog. How can you deliver what the Hawk with his mighty wings cannot deliver?"

"Strength is not necessarily the answer for every task."

The son of Kim-ana-u-eze was impressed with this answer, and he gave the letter to the Frog. "But if you are seeking to make a fool of me," he warned, "you will be very unhappy."

"You will see."

The Frog went to the well where the people of Lord Sun and Lady Moon came to get water. He jumped down the well and waited. After a while, the people of Lord Sun and Lady Moon came. They put a pitcher into the water, and Frog swam into the pitcher. They took the pitcher from the well filled with water, not realizing that Frog was at the bottom. They returned to the Palace of Lord Sun and Lady Moon in the sky. There, they went into a room, placed the pitcher in a corner, and left.

Frog leaped out of the pitcher, and, looking around the room, he saw a table, placed the letter

on it, then hid in the corner. Shortly, the Lord of the Sun came into the room and saw the letter on the table. He called his people and asked, "Where did this letter come from?"

"We do not know," they said.

He opened the letter and read it: "I, the son of Na Kim-ana-u-eze Kia Tumb'a Ndala, a man of earth, want to marry the daughter of Lord Sun and Lady Moon." Lord Sun put the letter away and told no one of its contents, for he could not understand how a man of the earth had delivered a letter to him.

Frog leaped back in the jug, and, when it was emptied, the water girls returned to the earth to refill it. When they arrived at the well, Frog leaped quietly out and hid until the water girls returned to the sky.

Many days passed, and the son of Kim-ana-u-eze heard nothing from Frog. So he went to look for him. "Did you deliver my letter?"

"I did," Frog said, "but they sent no answer in return."

"You lie! You did not go! I knew you would deceive me!"

Frog was afraid. "Trust me. Perhaps the Lord of the Sun will respond to your next letter."

The son of Kim-ana-u-eze left Frog in anger.

Six days passed before he decided he would give Frog one more chance, and he wrote another letter: "I wrote you, Lord Sun and Lady Moon. My letter was delivered, but you did not answer. You did not tell me whether you accept me or reject me." He went to Frog and gave him the letter. "I hope, for your sake, you return with an answer this time."

Frog went to the well, waited, and when the water girls came, he leaped into the jug and was thus transported to the sky where Lord Sun and Lady Moon lived. Once in the palace, he hid in the jug until the room was empty. Then he leaped out, placed the letter on the table, and returned to the corner.

Soon the Lord of the Sun passed through the room and saw the letter on the table. He opened it and read its contents. He called the water girls. "Are you carrying letters when you go to get the water?"

"Oh, no," they told him.

Lord Sun did not know whether he should believe them, but they had never given him the slightest cause to doubt their trustworthiness. So he decided to write a reply. "You may marry my daughter if you come with your first present. I wish to know you." He folded the letter and placed it on the table. Then he left the room.

Frog leaped to the table, got the letter, and leaped back into the jug. Shortly, someone came into the room and emptied the pitcher, and the water girls lifted it up and brought it back to earth.

Frog waited until evening and then took the letter to the son of Kim-ana-u-eze. "Who is it?" the son of Kim-ana-u-eze asked when he heard a knock at his door.

"It is I. Mainu, the frog."

"Come in."

Frog went in, gave him the letter, and left. The son of Kim-ana-u-eze opened the letter, and what he read made him happy. He took forty gold coins from his purse and wrote: "I have brought the first present. I await your word as to what you would find worthy of a wooing present." The son of Kim-ana-u-eze put the forty gold coins into a small pouch, sealed the letter, and waited until morning to give them to Frog.

Frog returned to the well, waited until the water girls came, and returned with them to the sky, hidden in the bottom of the water pitcher. They placed the pitcher in the corner, left the room, and Frog placed the letter and the pouch of money on the table and hid in the corner.

Soon Lord Sun came into the room, and when he read the letter and examined the gold coins, he was pleased. He looked all around the room for the one who had brought it, but saw no one. He smiled to himself, admiring the cleverness of his daughter's suitor. Lord Sun called Lady Moon, and when he showed her what their daughter's suitor had written and sent as a first present, she, too, was pleased. Lady Moon ordered a young hen to be cooked, so that he who sought their daughter would have something to eat. It was soon ready and was placed on the table. When the room was empty, Frog came out of the corner, ate the young hen, and returned to the corner.

Several hours later, Lord Sun came into the room and was pleased that the hen had been devoured, though he still had not seen who had devoured it. He sat down at the table and wrote another letter: "Your present was received. The amount of your wooing present shall be a sack of gold coins." He sealed the letter, placed it on the table, and left the room. Frog came out of the corner, took the letter, and leaped in the jug and went to sleep.

The next morning, the water girls came into the room, lifted the jug, and took it to earth. Frog waited until evening and then went to the home of the son of Kim-ana-u-eze, gave him the letter, and departed.

The son of Kim-ana-u-eze read the letter and

was pleased. Six days later he had gathered the sack of gold coins. "Here is the wooing present," he wrote. "Soon I will tell you on what day I will bring my wife to my home." He called Frog and gave him the letter and the sack of gold.

Frog went to the well, and soon he was in the pitcher of Lord Sun and Lady Moon being carried to the sky by the water girls. Once again, he waited until the room was empty and placed the letter and the sack of gold coins on the table.

Before long, Lord Sun came into the room and saw the letter and the sack of gold. He read the letter, examined the gold, and was pleased. He called Lady Moon, and she, too, was pleased. She ordered a young pig roasted for her daughter's husband-to-be. When it was ready, it was placed on the table. When the room was empty, Frog came out of the corner and ate it. Then he got back in the jug and went to sleep.

The next morning, the water girls returned to earth with the pitcher, Frog hiding quietly inside. That evening, he went to the home of the son of Kim-ana-u-eze and told him all that had happened. "Now you must choose the day when you wish to bring your bride home."

For twelve days, the son of Kim-ana-u-eze tried to find one of the animals who could go to the sky and bring his bride home. None of them could. The son of Kim-ana-u-eze went to Frog and told him. "There is nothing I can do, Frog."

"Leave it to me," Frog said.

"You have done much, Frog, and I thank you. But you cannot bring my bride home. You are too small."

"Strength is not the only virtue, son of Kim-ana-u-eze."

Frog went to the well and returned to the home of Lord Sun and Lady Moon as he had done many times before. He hid in the corner of the room until evening. When all was quiet, he quickly made his way through the palace until he came to the room where the daughter of the Sun and the Moon was sleeping. There he took out her eyes and tied them in a handkerchief. Then he went back to his corner and went to sleep.

The next morning, the Lord of the Sun was troubled when his daughter did not come to breakfast. He went to her room to see if she were ill.

"I cannot get up, father. I cannot see."

Lord Sun called Lady Moon, and they could not understand what was the matter. The day before, their daughter's eyes had sparkled like the night sky. Lord Sun called three messengers to him. "Go to Ngombo, the witch doctor, and tell him what has happened, and ask what we should do."

Before evening, they returned and said, "Ngombo said that she is not yet married. He whom she is to marry has put a spell upon her and said that if she does not come to him, she will die."

Lord Sun listened closely, and then he ordered everyone to get his daughter ready to meet her husband, and, come the morning, the messengers would take her to earth.

The next morning, Frog returned to earth in the pitcher of the water girls, and after they returned, he waited beside the well. That evening, the messengers descended to earth, the daughter of the Sun and the Moon with them. They left her beside the well and returned to the sky.

Frog returned the girl's eyes and led her to the house of the son of Kim-ana-u-eze. And thus the son of Kim-ana-u-eze married the daughter of the Sun and Moon, and, while they lived, they lived happily.

Jack and
the Devil's Daughter

Once there was a man who had two sons. One day when the sons were almost grown, the old man called them in. "I've decided to give you boys what you got coming to you right now. I don't want y'all hanging around the house waiting for me to die. So here." He gave each of them $1,ooo, which was their inheritance. "Now I don't want either one of you ever coming to me again for anything in the world. Do with the money what you want to, but if you end up broke, shame on you."

The first son, whose name was John, bought a little grocery store, got married, and settled down.

The other son, whose name was Jack, put the $1,000 in one pocket, a deck of cards in the other, and took off down the road. Jack was a natural-born gambler. Everybody else had to have bad luck, because Jack had all the good luck. There wasn't a card game in the world he couldn't play. And when the money started to hit the table, there wasn't anybody around who could beat Jack.

It was a very good thing that Jack was talented at gambling, because if he had had to work for a living, he would've died. Jack treated work like he treated his mama, and he wouldn't hit his mama a lick. His hands were still baby-soft. But don't let that fool you. If Jack had to, he could shoot out a flea's eye at 100 yards and cut a man so quick, the man would be afraid to bleed if Jack told him not to.

Well, this one day, Jack walked into this place and saw a man sitting by himself at a table. "You look like you might be a card player," Jack said to the man.

The man didn't say a word. He just nodded.

Jack sat down, shuffled the cards, and started dealing. Jack looked at his cards. The man looked at his and laid $100 on the table.

"Aw, man, I thought you wanted to gamble," Jack laughed, laying down $500 plus $100 to cover the man's bet.

The man didn't blink an eye. He laid down another $500 and raised Jack $300 more. Jack threw away two cards and pulled two more from the top of the deck. He laid down $300. "You ain't gon' take no cards?" Jack asked the man.

There was no response.

Jack shrugged. "It's your money you losing." He grinned and laid down three tens. The man spread three queens and a pair of deuces and took the money.

Jack laughed. "Well, you got lucky that time. Let's go 'round again."

They played another hand, and Jack lost all of his money. "Well, mister, you the best I ever run into. I guess the game's over, 'cause you got all my money."

The man spoke for the first time. "I'll bet you all the money on the table against your life."

Jack laughed. "Why not? I'm a gambling man, sure as you're born." Jack wasn't worried. Even if he lost the game, he knew he could out-cut, out-shoot, and out-fight any man around. So if the man did try to kill him, Jack had no doubt that he'd kill him first.

They played another hand and Jack lost. Then the man got up from the table and he stood fourteen feet tall. Jack was as scared as he could be. The man looked down at him and said in a deep voice, "My name is the Devil, and I live across the deep blue sea. I'm not going to kill you right now, because I like your style. If you get to my house by this time tomorrow, I'll spare you. If you don't, you're mine." And he disappeared.

Jack didn't know what he was going to do. He had sat there and played cards with the Devil. Wasn't no way in the world he could've won! The more he thought about it, the worse he felt. And the worse he felt, the more he thought about it.

An old man came in the place and saw Jack sitting there with tears rolling down his face. "What's the matter with you, son?"

"I played cards with the Devil, and he won. He said if I don't get to his house across the ocean by this time tomorrow, he's going to kill me."

The old man said, "You got problems. Ain't no doubt about that. There ain't but one thing that can cross the ocean to where the Devil live at."

"What's that?"

"The bald eagle. There's a bald eagle that comes down to the edge of the ocean every morning, washes in the water, and picks off the dead feathers. When she dips herself in the water the third time, she kinda rocks a little bit, then spreads her wings and takes off again. Now if you could be there with a yearling bull, after she dips in the water the third time, and then rocks, you jump on her back and she'll take you there."

"What's the yearling bull for?"

"She gets hungry going across the ocean, and every time she hollers, you give her some of the yearling bull and you'll be all right. If you don't, she'll eat you."

The next morning, Jack was there bright and early. Sure enough, he hadn't been there long when a bald eagle came flying from the other side of the ocean. Jack watched, and when she dipped herself in the water the third time and rocked a little bit, Jack jumped on her back, the yearling bull under his arm, and the bald eagle started climbing toward the sun.

They'd been flying for a short while when the eagle started twisting her head from side to side, and her blazing eyes lit up the northern sky and then the southern sky, and she hollered:

One-quarter 'cross the ocean!
Don't see nothing but blue water!

One-quarter 'cross the ocean!
Don't see nothing but blue water!

Jack got scared when he heard the eagle sing like that, and, instead of giving her just a piece of the yearling bull, he gave her all of it. The eagle swallowed it down and kept on flying.

After a while, the eagle twisted her head from side to side, and her blazing eyes lit up the northern sky and the southern sky, and she hollered:

Halfway 'cross the ocean!
Don't see nothing but blue water!

Halfway 'cross the ocean!
Don't see nothing but blue water!

Jack didn't have any meat left, but he was so scared that he tore off his leg and gave it to her. She swallowed that down and flew on. After a while, she twisted her head to one side, then the other, and her blazing eyes lit up the northern sky and the southern sky, and she hollered:

Three-quarters 'cross the ocean!
Don't see nothing but blue water!

Three-quarters 'cross the ocean!
Don't see nothing but blue water!

Jack tore off an arm and gave it to her. She swallowed that down and flew on. Pretty soon the eagle landed, and Jack jumped off and started down the road looking for the Devil's house. He didn't know exactly where the Devil lived, so he asked the first person he saw.

"It's the first big white house 'round the curve in the road," Jack was told.

He went on to the house and knocked on the door.

"Who's that?" a voice called out.

"One of the Devil's friends. One without an arm or a leg."

The Devil told his wife, "Reach behind the door and hand that fool an arm and a leg and let him in."

Jack put on the arm and leg and stepped in the house.

"Well," said the Devil, "I see you got here. You just in time for breakfast."

"That's good, 'cause I sure am hungry."

"I'm sure you are. Well, before you eat, I wonder if you'd do a little job for me."

"Be glad to help out," Jack said.

"Glad to hear it. I got a hundred acres of forest out back that I need cut down to keep the fires of Hell burning."

"A hundred acres, you say?"

"That ain't much for a man who played cards with the Devil."

"And you want me to do it before breakfast?"

"If you don't," the Devil said, "I'm going to take your life."

Jack picked up an axe and went out back. When he saw the 100 acres of trees, he knew that it would take 100 men working 100 years to cut all that forest down. It would take him a year just to cut one side of one tree. Jack had never seen trees that were so big and tall. Jack didn't need to take a second look at the trees to know that he was beat. So, instead of sitting down and worrying about it, Jack lay down and went to sleep.

Now the Devil had a daughter named Beulah Mae, and she had been peeping at Jack from the back room and had fallen in love with him. Nobody can tell why somebody falls in love with some-

body else. Maybe she fell in love with him because of the green suede shoes he had on. Maybe she liked the pink shirt he was wearing. Maybe she liked the way the sequins on his suit sparkled. Maybe she liked the way his gold tooth sparkled. Whatever it was, she was madly in love with Jack, and when she heard her father give Jack all that work to do, she knew that her father was simply looking for an excuse to kill him. She'd seen it happen before. But she liked Jack, and she didn't want it to happen to him. So she went out back and found Jack sleeping like Daniel in the lion's den.

"Don't you know my father's going to kill you if you don't get this work done?" she asked, waking him up.

"Who're you?" Jack asked, opening one eye.

"I'm Beulah Mae, the Devil's daughter."

Jack opened the other eye. "Well, Beulah Mae, I'm just glad your daddy let me live long enough to rest my eyes on you. Honey, you're prettier than a royal flush. You look as good as Aretha sounds."

Beulah Mae blushed. "Well, I'll help you get this forest cut. You just put your head in my lap and go back to sleep."

Jack didn't need a second invitation, and

when he went to sleep, Beulah Mae looked at the axe and sang:

> Axe cut on one side,
> Cut on the other.
> When one tree falls
> All fall together.

And just like that, the whole 100 acres of trees came down.

After a while, Beulah Mae woke Jack up, and he went into the house to get his breakfast.

"You all through?" the Devil asked.

Jack nodded. "Yeah, and it sho' gave me a good appetite, too."

The Devil went out back, and sure enough, the whole 100 acres was down. "Well, Jack," the Devil said when he came back in, "you're almost as good a man as I am."

Jack grinned. "Almost."

The Devil couldn't figure out how Jack had cut down that 100 acres of trees. No one had ever been able to do it, and he wasn't too sure that Jack had done it. "When you get through breakfast, I got another thing I want you to help me out on."

"What's that?"

"I got a well. It's a hundred feet deep and I want you to dip it dry. And when I say dry, I don't mean muddy. I mean dry! I want that well so dry I want to see dust in the bottom. And then I want you to bring me what's in the bottom of the well."

"Is that all?" Jack asked, without looking up from his breakfast.

"That's all for now."

Jack took his time finishing breakfast, because he knew it was going to be his last meal. Dip a well so dry that there'd be dust in the bottom. The Devil was out of his mind. Jack spent a couple of hours picking his teeth and then went on out to the well and looked it over. Sure enough. It was 100 feet deep, at least. Jack took one look at it, turned his back, and went and stretched out on the grass. The minute he shut his eyes, he was asleep.

In a little while, Beulah Mae came out and woke Jack up. "What did daddy ask you to do this time?"

Jack woke up. "That fool told me to dip that hundred-foot-deep well dry and dip it so dry that there'd be dust in the bottom. Then he said to bring him what was at the bottom. Honey, your daddy is stone crazy!"

"No, he's not. He's the Devil."

"He's the Devil, and he's stone crazy!"

"Well, don't you worry about it. Just put your head in my lap and finish taking your nap. I'll take care of this well." As soon as Jack was asleep, Beulah Mae took a dipper and started singing:

> Dipper, dipper,
> Dip one drop.
> When you dip one drop,
> Dip every drop.

And no sooner had she said it than the well was so dry you could see the dust pouring out of it. She called her pet bird to her and told it to fly down to the bottom of the well and bring her what was there.

After a while, she woke Jack up and gave him a ring. "Go give this to daddy. Mama dropped it in the well yesterday."

Jack went in the house and gave the ring to the Devil. "Hey, man. You got to tell your ol' lady to be careful about where she let that ring slip off her finger from now on."

The Devil was really mad now. Not only did Jack get everything done, but he had the nerve to come in bragging about it. But the Devil didn't let on that he was angry. "Jack, you're almost as smart as I am. I tell you what. I been looking for a good number-two man that I could train. I got one more job for you, and, if you do it, I'll make you my number-two man, plus you can marry my daughter, Beulah Mae."

"Well, that's mighty nice of you, Mr. Devil. What'cha want me to do?"

"I got a goose. I want you to go up to the tallest tree and pick all the feathers off the goose, bring me the goose and all the feathers when you get through. If one feather is missing, you're mine."

"Aw, is that all?"

"Don't forget. If one feather is missing, you're mine."

"Don't you worry about it, dude. Ain't gon' be no feathers missing. It oughta be obvious to you by now that I don't mess around."

Jack got the goose, tied him to a bush, and went to sleep on the other side of the bush. He was sure that even Beulah Mae couldn't save him this time. Beulah Mae came to him, and he told her what her father wanted him to do.

"Just put your head in my lap and go back to sleep." After a while, she woke him up and handed him all the feathers tied into a neat little bundle. "That was a hard one, Jack."

"Honey, you ain't told me nothing."

"Here're the feathers and the goose. Take 'em in to daddy."

Jack strutted into the house and gave the feathers and the goose to the Devil. "Now, where's your daughter?"

The Devil was so angry, he wanted to kill Jack on the spot. Instead, he called Beulah Mae. "This is the man I've picked out for you to marry, Beulah Mae. He's going to be my assistant."

"That's nice, daddy."

The Devil noticed how she was looking at him, and how he was looking at her, and he knew who had done all the work. His own daughter, Beulah Mae Devil, had betrayed him.

"Jack, you and Beulah Mae can have that little pink stucco house down the road."

"Thank you, Devil. I sure appreciate all you've done for me."

Jack and Beulah Mae went to their house and had a big supper, and, after they did the dishes, went to bed. 'Way over in the night, Beulah Mae woke Jack up. "Jack! Jack! Wake up! Daddy's on his way here to kill you."

Jack woke up, but he didn't hear anything. "How do you know? I don't hear nothing."

"I'm the Devil's daughter, ain't I? The same powers he got, I got. And I can hear him coming. Now get up and go to the barn. Daddy's got two horses that can jump a thousand miles at a jump. One of them is named Hallowed-Be-Thy-Name.

The other one is called Thy-Kingdom-Come. You hitch 'em to the buckboard so we can get out of here."

When the Devil got to the house, he found that Jack and Beulah Mae had gone. He ran to the barn to get his two fast horses, and they were gone. Then he got his bull, which could jump 500 miles at a jump, and he was after 'em.

The Devil was tearing up some road, and every time the bull jumped, the Devil would holler: "Hallowed-Be-Thy-Name! Thy-King-dom-Come!" And the horses would fall to their knees when they heard his voice, and the Devil would be steady gaining.

"He's going to catch us," Beulah Mae said. "Jack, you get out and draw your feet backwards nine steps, throw some sand over your left shoulder, and let's go."

Jack did what she'd told him, and the horses were off again, 1,000 miles at a jump.

"Hallowed-Be-Thy-Name! Thy-Kingdom-Come!" the Devil hollered.

The horses fell to their knees again, and the Devil was getting closer.

"It's too late," Beulah Mae said. "He's going to catch us."

"Well, what we gon' do?"

"I'll turn into a lake, and I'll turn you into a duck swimming on the lake." She tried to turn Jack into a duck, but he was so tough that he wouldn't turn into nothing.

"Oh, Lord! What we gon' do, Beulah Mae, honey?"

"That's O.K. I'll turn myself into the lake and the horses into ducks, and you be a hunter." She pulled a gun out of the air and handed it to him.

She had scarcely done it when the Devil came by on his bull, and he was steady trucking. He went on by them, five hundred miles a jump. As soon as he was out of sight, Beulah Mae turned back into herself and turned the ducks back into horses, and they started off in another direction at 1,000 miles a jump.

It wasn't long, though, before the Devil realized he'd been tricked, and he came back, got on their trail, and was after them. "Hallowed-Be-Thy-Name! Thy-Kingdom-Come!" And the horses fell to their knees.

Beulah Mae jumped out of the buckboard, pulled a thorn off a rosebush, and stuck it in the ground.

> When I plant one thorn,
> I plant 'em all.

Grow thorns!
Three thousand miles high,
Three thousand miles wide,
Three thousand miles long.
Grow thorns!

And no sooner had she said it than the biggest thornbush the world has even seen grew in that place.

When the Devil got to the wall of thorns, there was nothing he could do. By the time he had cast the spell to make the thorns disappear, Jack and Beulah Mae were riding across the ocean on the back of the eagle. Jack took Beulah Mae to Harlem, and they settled down. Jack went into business at the store with his brother, selling numbers. They raised a big family, and, whenever you hear a mother saying to her child, "Boy, you got the Devil in you," more than likely it's one of Jack and Beulah Mae's grandchildren.

Heroes

High John the Conqueror

Way back during slavery time, there was a man named John. High John the Conqueror, they called him. And he was what you call a *man*. Now some folks say he was a big man, but the way I heard it, he wasn't no bigger than average height and didn't look no different than the average man. Didn't make any difference, though. He was what you call a *be* man—be here when the hard times come, and be here when the hard times are gone.

No matter how much the white folks put on him, John always survived.

John lived on this plantation in Mississippi. I'm not quite sure whereabouts in Mississippi, but it must've been on one of them cotton plantations up in what they call the Delta. John lived on one of them bad plantations. They had plantations so bad up in there, and the white folks was so mean, that the rattlesnakes wouldn't even bite 'em. 'Fraid they'd poison themselves. Snakes only bit niggers. White folks was so mean up there, they'd shoot a nigger just to bet on whether the body would fall frontwards or backwards. And then they'd go whup the dead nigger's mama if the body fell the wrong way.

That's the kind of plantation John lived on. But it didn't bother John none. He was a *be* man. Wasn't no disputing that. High John loved living, and, although he was a slave, he made up in his mind that he was gon' do as much living and as little slaving as he could. He used to break the hoes—accidentally, of course. Set ol' massa's barn on fire. Accidentally, of course. He always had a hard time getting to the field on time, and when he did get there, somehow the mule would accidentally tromp down a whole row of cotton before the boss man knew what was happening.

Ol' massa was never sure, though, whether or not John was doing all this on purpose, because John would work real hard some years and make a good crop. The next year, though, it seemed like everything he touched got destroyed. But the following year, he'd pick more cotton than anybody ever thought possible. So the white folks were never sure just whose side John was on. And you better believe that that was the way John wanted it.

Well, it was after one of those seasons when John had really worked, and ol' massa decided he would reward John for it. Maybe it would encourage him to do good work all the time, massa thought. So he gave John an ol' mule and a patch of ground so John could raise a few vegetables of his own. John thanked massa, but the last thing John wanted was a mule of his own. Why should he have to raise his own vegetables when he could take massa's? Stealing was what you did if you took something from another black person. Anything you took from white folks was yours to begin with, because everything they had they got because of your work.

So John really didn't want the ol' mule. All it meant was that massa would expect to see him out there plowing up that little patch of ground, and John had had enough of work for a while. With all the work he'd done this year, he figured on not working hard for the next five. So he started thinking how he was going to get rid of the mule massa had given him.

Bright and early the next morning, John went down to the barn to hitch up his mule. He decided to hitch up massa's best mule to his mule to make the plowing easier, and he went on out to the field and began plowing. Now you know how stubborn mules are. There're some niggers like mules. Won't do right for doing wrong. Well, these were some sho' nuf' nigger mules, and every time the mules would balk, John would take his whip and hit massa's mule. WHACK! "Get up there, Miss Anne!" He'd nicknamed massa's mule Miss Anne and he'd hit that mule as hard as he could. WHACK! "What's wrong with you, Miss Anne! Act like you got some sense!" WHACK! But he never would hit his own mule. If John's mule acted like it was having a hard time, he'd stop, and fan it, and give it a sip of Kool-Aid.

Well, one of them ol' Uncle Tom niggers come by. You know the kind I mean. One of them house niggers who wore massa's hand-me-down clothes. Them was the kind of niggers that would sell their grandmama if it meant they'd get a word

of praise from the white folks. Them was the kind of niggers that just loved white folks. They wanted to be white folks so bad that they always tried to walk in the shade. Walking in the shade wouldn't make 'em white, but at least they wouldn't get no blacker. Them kind of niggers loved ol' massa so much that if massa's house caught on fire, the house nigger would say, "Massa, *our* house is on fire." House nigger barely had a house. If massa was sick, house nigger would come 'round and say, "Massa, *we* sick, ain't we?" And you know that's how they are, 'cause I couldn't make up nothing like that.

From what I've heard, we got some house niggers with us today. If the people are talking about black power, it's the house nigger who runs down to the white folks and says, "Boss, Tom, Sally, Bob, and James are up there talking about this here black power!" If the folks are talking about getting them some guns to defend themselves from the police, the house nigger goes and tells the police. Living with a house nigger is worse than picking up a hungry rattlesnake and putting it inside your shirt.

At any rate, it was one of them house niggers who came by and saw High John beating on massa's mule. Great God a-Mighty! He took off for the big house. "Massa! Massa!"

"Roy, what's wrong with you?"

"Oh Lawd, massa! Oh Lawd! You oughta see what I just seen. Oh Lawd, massa!"

"Well, nigger, stop all this nonsense and tell me what it is."

"Massa, John is down there in the field with your best mule, and he's whipping it like whipping is going out of style. Massa, you got to do something before John kills our mule."

You have to understand that John was a field nigger. John had never set foot in massa's house and wouldn't have if he'd had the opportunity. Only way John would've gone in the big house was through the window one night with a knife in his hand. John worked in the fields, and if massa's house caught on fire, you could be sure that John had set it afire and was down behind the barn praying for a big wind. And if massa got sick, John was praying he'd die. I understand, too, that we got some field niggers running around today. Praise the Lord!

Well, ol' massa went marching down to the fields to see if what Roy was saying was true. He got there, and ol' John was trying to carve his initials on that mule's backside. WHACKITY, WHACK, WHACK, WHACK, WHACKITY! John was making that whip talk like Martin Luther King, Jr. preaching.

Ol' massa turned right red in the face. You

know how white folks look when they get mad. "John! What you think you doing?"

"Massa, I'm glad you come by, 'cause I'm just plumb wore out trying to beat some sense into this mule of yours. I say 'Gee,' and he go 'Haw.' I say 'Haw,' and he go 'Gee.' I just can't do a thing with your mule, boss."

Massa didn't know what to say for a minute, 'cause he'd expected John to be apologizing. "Well, J-J-John, what're you doing with my mule, anyway? You didn't ask me if you could use it."

"Well, I figured you wouldn't mind a bit once you saw the vegetables I was gon' be bringing you to put on your table."

For a minute, ol' massa was sorry he'd ever laid eyes on a nigger. They were Excedrin Headache Number One. Wasn't no doubt about it. "Well, John, if I catch you beating on my mule one more time, I'm going to kill your mule."

"What's that, massa?"

"I said, you beat mine, I'm going to kill yours."

"Well, massa, if you do, I bet I'll beat you making money."

Massa just looked at John, thinking he must've lost his mind. "I don't know what nonsense you talking about, John, but hit my mule one more time, and your mule is going to be dead."

Massa wasn't out of sight when ol' John started in on Miss Anne one more time. WHACKITY, WHACK, WHACK, WHACKITY, WHACKITY, WHACK! I mean John just laid it on her that time. Massa came tearing back to the field.

"I told you, John. I told you." And he pulled out his knife and cut John's mule's throat.

John shrugged his shoulders. "Well, I guess I got to beat you making money."

Now what massa didn't know was that John was a conjure man. I mean John could conjure anything. He was even better than Aunt Caroline Dye, and you know she was one of the best. John could cast spells and cast 'em away. He could tell when a man was gonna die and a baby be born. He could tell when a woman was doing what she wasn't supposed to and a man was doing what he wasn't supposed to. And, if John had a good reason, he could make the birds sing at midnight and the dew fall at noon on a hot summer day. High John was so famous that they even got a root named after him now, called the John-the-Conqueror root, and it's the most powerful root there is. Only thing more powerful than the John-the-Conqueror root is a Black Cat Bone, and John had one of them.

Well, John cut off the mule's skin, dried it,

and went into town to make some money. He sat down on the lawn around the courthouse and started shaking his muleskin. "Fortune telling! Fortune telling!"

A white man came up and said, "Nigger, can you tell fortunes?"

"Yes, suh."

"If you tell mine, I'll give you ten dollars."

John shook the muleskin three times, held it up to his eye, shook it again, threw some dust on it, shook the dust off, and looked at the muleskin again. "Oh Lawd!"

"Nigger, what're you moaning about?"

"Naw. It can't be."

"Nigger, what're you talking about? What do you see on that muleskin?"

John shook his head. "Let me examine this real close." And he turned the muleskin upside down. "Say the same thing this way, too."

John slowly folded the muleskin. "Boss, I just can't tell you. You wouldn't like it."

"Nigger, if you don't tell me, I'll kill you."

John chuckled. "You can do that if you want to, but then you never would find out."

"I'll give you a hundred dollars."

John thought for a minute. "Boss, I'm just telling you what I saw on the muleskin. This is the muleskin talking, not me."

"O.K. O.K. Now what'd that muleskin say?"

"Well, the muleskin said that you shouldn't go home early today. The muleskin say if you don't go home early, you won't see your wife and best friend sitting in the house all by themselves. And the muleskin say they ain't reading the Bible to each other."

The white man pulled out his gun. "Nigger, you lying, and I'm gon' blow your head off."

John just looked at him. "I knew it. White folks don't want to hear the truth. Just want to hear what they want to hear. You asked me and I told you. Now you want to blame me for what your wife is doing."

The white man slowly put the gun away. "Nigger, if you lying, I'm coming back here and kill you."

"Just be sure you bring a hundred dollars with you when you come."

Well, the white man took off for home, and just like John said, his wife and his best friend were there not reading the Bible. The white man shot both of 'em and came back and gave John the money.

John went on back to the plantation after telling a few more fortunes, and, as he was going to his house, he saw ol' massa. "Hey there, massa!"

"What you so happy about, John?"

"I told you if you killed my mule, I'd beat you making money." And John pulled out enough money to paper a house with. Of course, there was a whole lot of inflation then, so he didn't have more than fifty dollars, but it looked good, anyway.

Massa's eyes got real big. He had more money than he knew what to do with, but you know how greedy some white folks are. They got cash registers instead of souls. "Uh, John. You think if I kill my mule, I could make some money?"

"Oh, massa. I know you could."

Massa ran down to the barn, killed his mule, and skinned it. Next morning, he was in town bright and early. "Muleskin for sale! Muleskin for sale!"

"Give you two bits for it," one man said.

"Two bits! This muleskin is worth a hundred dollars."

All day, massa went around yelling, "Muleskin for sale," and folks thought he had lost his mind. When sundown came, massa threw the muleskin in a ditch and came home, angry at John.

"Well, massa, I didn't tell you to go try to sell no muleskin for a hundred dollars. Why, anybody knows a muleskin ain't worth more than two bits. What's wrong, massa? These niggers about done drove you crazy. That's what it is. These niggers would drive St. Peter to sin. You need a rest. You ain't thinking straight."

Well, massa was so mad he could've killed John, but he couldn't see a way he could do it and make a profit, so he let him live. A week or so later, massa just happened to be talking to another slave-owner.

"I got a nigger on my plantation that can whup any nigger in the world," this slave-owner said.

"Can't whup my nigger John."

"I got twenty-five thousand dollars say he can."

"It's a bet," John's owner said. "We'll have the match in town a month from today."

Massa couldn't wait for the match. He knew that John was probably going to get killed, and massa didn't mind losing $25,000 for the pleasure of seeing it.

Well, the news spread around the state quicker than hoof-and-mouth disease. It was going to be a match between the two baddest niggers in Mississippi. All the white folks was planning on coming. The Governor had announced he was coming and bringing his family. White folks didn't like nothing better than to see two niggers in the ring, fighting each other until they both fell out.

"Well, John," massa said one day, "you getting ready for the match?"

John was stretching out on the grass eating some chicken. "I'm ready, massa."

"John! Where'd you get that chicken leg from?"

"Strangest thing, massa. Last night, this chicken just walked in my house, and I was trying to chase it out, you know, and that chicken got so scared that it jumped in this skillet of hot grease I had on the fire. And before I could do a thing, it was all fried. So I thanked the Lord for sending a chicken to a poor, honest, colored man. You know something, massa?" John asked, throwing the chicken bone on massa's hat brim. "The Lord sure takes care of you when you live right."

Massa didn't say a word, but stalked off angrily. He couldn't wait to see John get a good beating.

Well, the day of the match came, and white folks were there from everywhere. There were white folks there from Hang-a-Nigger, Mississippi. And there were white folks there from Cut-a-Nigger, Alabama, and Burn-a-Nigger, Georgia, and even some white folks from Co-opt-a-Nigger, New

York. The Governor and his wife and daughter were there. The Lieutenant Governor and his family was there. The Sergeant Governor and his family. The Corporal Governor and his family. There was so many white folks there, it looked like a lynching party.

About an hour before the match was to start, in come the plantation owner with his nigger Andy. Now, let me tell you, this was one big nigger. He was so big and strong, they had him tied with chains. He was snorting and growling and carrying on so that they had to chain him to one of the pillars of the courthouse. He was so big that he had to stoop down at nights to let the moon go by. Four white ladies fainted when they saw him. When John's massa saw him, he began to feel sorry he'd made the bet. He looked at that nigger Andy and could just see John getting pulverized. John deserved a good beating, but nothing like what he was going to get.

Well, about ten minutes before match time, in come John. And John was dressed like he was going to his own funeral. I mean, he was clean! Had him on a pair of black patent leather shoes with spats. Some red trousers with a red coat, a white shirt, and a black string tie. Over his arm was a hand-carved cane studded with diamonds. He was wearing a Stetson hat and walking real slow, tipping his hat to everybody. John diddy-bopped down the aisle speaking to all the white folks. "How you do, boss. It's good to see you. Haven't seen you since you sold my mama." "How you do, suh? Last time I saw you was the time you whipped my sister and rubbed the cuts with vinegar. That was to keep her from getting lockjaw." John was as polite as he could be. A perfect gentleman.

After John had finished greeting all the white folks, he stepped out in the center and looked around. He pretended like he hadn't even seen Andy, who was snorting like he had swallowed a box of snuff. John looked around until he spied the Governor and walked over to him as fast as he could go, looking mean, mean, mean. John crawled over the Governor's wife, stepped on the Governor, and hauled off and slapped the Governor's daughter. POW! He hit that white girl all upside the head. He hit that girl so hard that her blonde hair turned brown. He hit her so hard she was cross-eyed for the rest of her life. POW! He smacked her again! "Girl, didn't I tell you to stay at home and not come out here today! What do you mean disobeying me?" POW! He smacked her one more time.

Well, when that nigger Andy saw John hit that white girl, he started getting away so fast that he pulled the courthouse down, broke his chains and, from what I heard, he didn't stop running until he got to Canada. Andy knew he couldn't whup John, 'cause if John was bad enough to slap a white woman, John was bad enough to whup him.

The white folks were kind of upset about John slapping that white woman until they realized that he'd simply outsmarted everybody. Then they fell out laughing. Especially the ones who had bet on John. Massa wasn't mad, 'cause the Governor's daughter had said one time that his son wasn't good enough for her to marry. But the Governor was kind of ticked off until ol' massa slipped him half of the $25,000, at which point the Governor told his daughter to shut up all that screaming and hollering, or he was going to smack her one time himself.

John went on back to the plantation, and, even though he'd won massa all that money, he still had to get out in the fields and work the next day. John couldn't see why, so he went in the barn and broke all the plows, the hoes, poured water in the cotton seed, broke the mules' legs, told the house nigger to go tell it, and then stretched out under a big sycamore tree, put his hat over his face to keep the flies off, and went to sleep.

"John! You went too far this time!" massa hollered. "You just went too far this time, and I'm going to kill you!"

John didn't even take the hat off his face. "Kill me, and I'll beat you making money."

"Not this time, nigger."

Massa shoved John in a gunny sack and drug him down to the river to throw him in. But he'd forgotten his weights and had to go back to the big house to get them. While he was gone, some of the other field niggers, who'd been watching all along, came out of the woods, untied the sack, and let John out. They filled the sack with stones, and when massa came back with his weights, he threw a sack of stones in the river. By that time, though, John was home, finishing his nap.

Later that afternoon, he got up, grabbed his muleskin and went into town to tell fortunes. Long about six that afternoon, he came back to the plantation, money just jingling in his pocket.

"John? Is that you?" massa said when he saw him.

"I told you if you killed me, I'd beat you making money."

"John?"

"Yes, massa."

"John, you think if I let you kill me, I could make some money?"

John's face was very serious as he said, "Massa, I *know* you could."

John shoved ol' massa in a gunny sack and tied it up. John called to the other field niggers, and they didn't forget their weights. They carried the sack down to the river, and, just as they were getting ready to throw it in, massa called out, "You sure I'm gon' make some money, John?"

"Massa, I *know* you is," John called back, as ol' massa hit the water and sank.

And that's the story of High John the Conqueror.

Stagolee

Stagolee was, undoubtedly and without question, the baddest nigger that ever lived. Stagolee was so bad that the flies wouldn't even fly around his head in the summertime, and snow wouldn't fall on his house in the winter. He was bad, jim.

Stagolee grew up on a plantation in Georgia, and by the time he was two, he'd decided that he wasn't going to spend his life picking cotton and working for white folks. Uh-uh. And when he was five, he left. Took off down the road, his guitar on his back, a deck of cards in one pocket and a .44 in the other. He figured that he didn't need nothing else. When the women heard him whup the blues on the guitar he could have whichever one he laid his mind on. Whenever he needed money, he could play cards. And whenever somebody tried to mess with him, he had his .44. So he was ready. A man didn't need more than that to get along with in the world.

By the time Stack was grown, his reputation had spread around the country. It got started one night in one of them honky-tonks down there in Alabama, and Stagolee caught some dude trying to deal from the bottom of the deck. Ol' Stack pulled out his .44 and killed him dead, right there on the spot. Then he moved the dead guy over to the center of the room and used the body as a card table. Another time, something similar happened, and Stack pulled the body over next to him, so a buddy of his, who was kinda short, would have something to sit on. Didn't take long for the word to get around that this was one bad dude! Even white folks didn't mess with Stagolee.

Well, this one time, Stagolee was playing cards with a dude they called Billy Lyons. Billy Lyons was one of them folk who acted like they

were a little better than anybody else. He'd had a little education, and that stuff can really mess your mind up. Billy Lyons had what he called a "scientific method" of cardplaying. Stagolee had the "nigger method." So they got to playing, and, naturally, Stagolee was just taking all of Billy Lyons's money, and Billy got mad. He got so mad that he reached over and knocked Stagolee's Stetson hat off his head and spit in it.

What'd he do that for? He could've done almost anything else in the world, but not that. Stack pulled his .44, and Billy started copping his plea. "Now, listen here, Mr. Stagolee. I didn't mean no harm. I just lost my head for a minute. I was wrong, and I apologize." He reached down on the ground, picked up Stack's Stetson, brushed it off, and put it back on his head. "I didn't mean no harm. See, the hat's all right. I put it back on your head." Billy was tomming like a champ, but Stack wasn't smiling. "Don't shoot me. Please, Mr. Stagolee! I got two children and a wife to support. You understand?"

Stack said, "Well, that's all right. The Lawd'll take care of your children. I'll take care of your wife." And, with that, Stagolee blowed Billy Lyons away. Stagolee looked at the body for a minute and then went off to Billy Lyons's house and told Mrs. Billy that her husband was dead and he was moving in. And that's just what he did, too. Moved in.

Now there was this new sheriff in town, and he had gotten the word about Stagolee, but this sheriff was a sho' nuf' cracker. He just couldn't stand the idea of Stagolee walking around like he was free—not working, not buying war bonds, cussing out white folks. He just couldn't put up with it, so, when he heard that Stagolee had shot Billy Lyons, he figured that this was his chance.

Sheriff told his deputies, said, "All right, men. Stagolee killed a man tonight. We got to get him."

The deputies looked at him. "Well, sheriff. Ain't nothing wrong with killing a man every now and then," said one.

"It's good for a man's health," added another.

"Well," said the sheriff, "that's all right for a white man, but this is a nigger."

"Now, sheriff, you got to watch how you talk about Stagolee. He's one of the leaders of the community here. You just can't come in here and start talking about one of our better citizens like that."

The sheriff looked at them. "I believe you men are afraid. Afraid of a nigger!"

Deputies thought it over for half a second. "Sheriff. Let's put it this way. We have a healthy respect for Stagolee. A long time ago, we struck ton

a bargain with him. We promised him that if he let us alone, we'd let him alone. And everything has worked out just fine."

"Well, we're going to arrest Stagolee," the sheriff said. "Get your guns, and let's go."

The deputies stood up, took their guns, and laid 'em on the shelf. "Sheriff, if you want Stagolee, well, you can arrest him by yourself." And they went on out the door and over to the undertaker's parlor and told him to start making a coffin for the sheriff.

When all the other white folks heard what the sheriff was going to do, they ran over to talk to him. "Sheriff, you can't go around disturbing the peace." But couldn't nobody talk no sense into him.

Now Stagolee heard that the sheriff was looking for him, and, being a gentleman, Stagolee got out of bed, told Mrs. Billy he'd be back in a little while, and went on down to the bar. He'd barely gotten the first drink down when the sheriff came stepping through the door.

He walked over to the bartender. "Barkeep? Who's that man down at the other end of the bar? You know there's a law in this town against drinking after midnight. Who is that?"

Bartender leaned over the counter and whispered in his ear, "Don't talk so loud. That's Stagolee. He drinks when he gets thirsty and he's generally thirsty after midnight."

Sheriff walked over to Stagolee. Stagolee didn't even look around. Sheriff pulled out his gun. Stack still didn't look around. Sheriff fired a couple of shots in the air. Stagolee poured himself another drink and threw it down. Finally, the sheriff said, "Stagolee, I'm the sheriff, and I'm white. Ain't you afraid?"

Stagolee turned around slowly. "You may be the sheriff, and you may be white, but you ain't Stagolee. Now deal with that."

The sheriff couldn't even begin to figure it out, no less deal with it, so he fell back in his familiar bag. "I'm placing you under arrest for the murder of Billy Lyons."

"You and what army? And it bet' not be the United States Army, 'cause I whupped them already."

"Me and this army," the sheriff growled, jabbing the pistol in Stack's ribs.

Before the sheriff could take another breath, Stagolee hit him upside the head and sent him flying across the room. Stagolee pulled out his gun, put three bullets in him, put his gun away, had

another drink, and was on his way out the door
before the body hit the floor.

The next day, Stagolee went to both of the
funerals to pay his last respects to the sheriff and
Billy Lyons, and then he settled down to living
with Mrs. Billy. She really didn't mind too much.
All the women knew how good-looking Stack
was. And he was always respectful to women, always had plenty of money, and, generally, he
made a good husband, as husbands go. Stagolee had
one fault, though. Sometimes he drank too much.
About once a month, Stagolee would buy up all
the available liquor and moonshine in the county
and proceed to get wasted, and when Stagolee
got wasted, he got totally wasted.

The new sheriff waited until one of those
nights when Stagolee was so drunk he was stag-
gering in his sleep, and he was lying flat in the bed.
If Judgment Day had come, the Lord would have
had to postpone it until Stagolee had sobered up.
Otherwise, the Lord might've ended up getting
Gabriel shot and his trumpet wrapped around his
head. When the sheriff saw Stagolee that drunk,
he went and got together the Ku Klux Klan
Alumni Association, which was every white man
in four counties. After the sheriff had assured
them that Stagolee was so drunk he couldn't wake

up, they broke in the house just as bad as you please. They had the lynching rope all ready, and they dropped it around his neck. The minute that rope touched Stack's neck, he was wide awake and stone cold sober. When white folks saw that, they were falling over each other getting out of there. But Stack was cool. He should've been. He invented it.

"Y'all come to hang me?"

The sheriff said that that was so. Stagolee stood up, stretched, yawned, and scratched himself a couple of times. "Well, since I can't seem to get no sleep, let's go and get this thing over with so I can get on back to bed."

They took him on out behind the jail where the gallows was built. Stagolee got up on the scaffold, and the sheriff dropped the rope around his neck and tightened it. Then the hangman opened up on the trap door, and there was Stack, swinging ten feet in the air, laughing as loud as you ever heard anybody laugh. They let him hang there for a half-hour, and Stagolee was still laughing.

"Hey, man! This rope is ticklish."

The white folks looked at each other and realized that Stack's neck just wouldn't crack. So they cut him down, and Stagolee went back home and went back to bed.

After that, the new sheriff left Stagolee in peace, like he should've done to begin with.

Stagolee lived on and on, and that was his big mistake. 'Cause Stagolee lived so long, he started attracting attention up in Heaven. One day, St. Peter was looking down on the earth, and he happened to notice Stack sitting on the porch picking on the guitar. "Ain't that Stagolee?" St. Peter said to himself. He took a closer look. "That's him. That's him. Why, that nigger should've been dead a long time ago." So St. Peter went and looked it up in the record book, and, sure enough, Stagolee was supposed to have died thirty years before.

St. Peter went to see the Lord.

"What's going on, St. Peter?"

"Oh, ain't nothing shaking, Lord. Well, that's not totally true. I was just checking out earth, and there's a nigger down there named Stagolee who is way overdue for a visit from Death."

"Is that so?"

"It's the truth, Lord."

"Well, we have to do something about that." The Lord cleared his throat a couple of times and hollered out, "HEY DEATH! HEEEEY, DEATH!"

Now Death was laying up down in the barn catching up on some sleep, 'cause he was tired.

Having to make so many trips to Vietnam was wearing him out, not to mention everywhere else in the world. He just couldn't understand why dying couldn't be systematized. He'd tried his best to convince God either to get a system to dying or get him some assistants. He'd proposed that, say, on Mondays, the only dying that would be done would be, say, in France, Germany, and a few other countries. Tuesday it'd be some other countries, and on like that. That way, he wouldn't have to be running all over the world twenty-four hours a day. But the Lord had vetoed the idea. Said it sounded to him like Death just wanted an excuse to eventually computerize the whole operation. Death had to admit that the thought had occurred to him. He didn't know when he was going to catch up on all the paperwork he had to do. A computer would solve everything. And now, just when he was getting to sleep, here come the Lord waking him up.

So Death got on his pale white horse. He was so tired of riding a horse he didn't know what to do. He'd talked to God a few months ago about letting him get a helicopter or something. But the Lord just didn't seem to understand. Death rode on off down through the streets of Heaven, and when folks heard him coming, they closed their doors, 'cause even in Heaven, folks were afraid of Death. And that was the other thing. Death was mighty lonely. Didn't nobody talk to him, and he was getting a little tired of it. He wished the Lord would at least let him wear a suit and tie and look respectable. Maybe then he could meet some nice young angel and raise a family. The Lord had vetoed that idea, too.

"What took you so long, Death?"

"Aw, Lord. I was trying to get some sleep. You just don't realize how fast folks are dying these days."

"Don't tell me you gon' start complaining again."

"I'm sorry, Lord, but I'd like to see you handle the job as well as I do with no help, no sleep, no wife, no nothing."

"Well, I got a special job for you today."

"Can't wait until tomorrow?"

"No, it can't wait, Death! Now hush up. There's a man down in Fatback, Georgia, named Stagolee. You should've picked him up thirty years ago, and I want you to send me a memo on why you didn't."

"Well, I got such a backlog of work piled up."

"I don't want to have to be doing your job

for you. You get the lists every day from the Record Bureau. How come you missed this one? If he's escaped for thirty years, who knows who else has been living way past their time. Speaking of folks living past their time, St. Peter, have the librarian bring me all the files on white folks. Seems to me that white folks sho' done outlived their time. Anyway, Death, go on down there and get Stagolee."

Death headed on down to earth. A long time ago, he used to enjoy the ride, but not anymore. There were so many satellites and other pieces of junk flying around through the air that it was like going through a junkyard barefooted. So he didn't waste any time getting on down to Fatback, Georgia.

Now on this particular day, Stagolee was sitting on the porch, picking the blues on the guitar, and drinking. All of a sudden, he looked up and saw this pale-looking white cat in this white sheet come riding up to his house on a white horse. "We ain't never had no Klan in the daytime before," Stagolee said.

Death got off his horse, pulled out his address book, and said, "I'm looking for Stagolee Booker T. Washington Nicodemus Shadrack Nat Turner Jones."

"Hey, baby! You got it down pat! I'd forgotten a couple of them names myself."

"Are you Stagolee Booker T. Wash—"

"You ain't got to go through the thing again. I'm the dude. What's going on?"

"I'm Death. Come with me."

Stagolee started laughing. "You who?"

"I'm Death. Come on, man. I ain't got all day."

"Be serious."

Death looked at Stagolee. No one had ever accused him of joking before. "I *am* serious. It's your time to die. Now come on here!"

"Man, you ain't bad enough to mess with me."

Death blinked his eyes. He'd never run up on a situation like this before. Sometimes folks struggled a little bit, but they didn't refuse. "Stagolee, let's go!" Death said in his baddest voice.

"Man, you must want to get shot."

Death thought that one over for a minute. Now he didn't know how to handle this situation, so he reached in his saddlebags and pulled out his *Death Manual*. He looked up *resistance* and read what it said, but wasn't a thing in there about what to do when somebody threatens you. Then he looked up *guns*, but that wasn't listed. He looked under everything he could think of, but nothing

was of any help. So he went back to the porch.
"You coming or not, Stagolee?"

Stagolee let one of them .44 bullets whistle
past ol' Death's ear, and Death got hot. Death
didn't waste no time getting away from there.
Before he was sitting in the saddle good, he had
made it back to Heaven.

"Lord! You must be trying to get me killed."

"Do what? Get you killed? Since when could
you die?"

"Don't matter, but that man Stagolee you just
sent me after took a shot at me. Now listen here,
Lord, if you want that man dead, you got to get
him yourself. I am not going back after him. I
knew there was some reason I let him live thirty
years too long. I'd heard about him on the grape-
vine and, for all I care, he can live three hundred
more years. I am not going back—"

"O.K. O.K. You made your point. Go on back
to sleep." After Death had gone, God turned to St.
Peter and asked, "We haven't had any new appli-
cations for that job recently?"

"You must be joking."

"Well, I was just checking." The Lord lit a
cigar. "Pete, looks like I'm going to have to use
one of my giant death thunderbolts to get that
Stagolee."

"Looks that way. You want me to tell the work crew?"

The Lord nodded, and St. Peter left. It took 3,412 angels 14 days, 11 hours, and 32 minutes to carry the giant death thunderbolt to the Lord, but he just reached down and picked it up like it was a toothpick.

"Uh, St. Peter? How you spell Stagolee?"

"Lord, you know everything. You're omnipotent, omiscient, omni—"

"You better shut up and tell me how to spell Stagolee."

St. Peter spelled it out for him, and the Lord wrote it on the thunderbolt. Then he blew away a few clouds and put his keen eye down on the earth. "Hey, St. Peter. Will you look at all that killing down there? I ain't never seen nothing like it."

"Lord, that ain't Georgia. That's Vietnam."

The Lord put his great eye across the world. "Tsk, tsk, tsk. Look at all that sin down there. Women wearing hardly no clothes at all. Check that one out with the black hair, St. Peter. Look at her! Disgraceful! Them legs!"

"LORD!"

And the Lord put his eye on the earth and

went on across the United States—Nevada, Utah, Colorado, Kansas, Missouri—

"Turn right at the Mississippi River, Lord!"

The Lord turned right and went on down into Tennessee.

"Make a left at Memphis, Lord!"

The Lord turned left at Memphis and went on up through Nashville and on down to Chattanooga into Georgia. Atlanta, Georgia. Valdosta. Rolling Stone, Georgia, until he got way back out in the woods to Fatback. He let his eye go up and down the country roads until he saw Stagolee sitting on the porch.

"That's him, Lord! That's him!"

And the Great God Almighty, the God of Nat Turner and Rap Brown, the God of Muddy Waters and B.B. King, the God of Aretha Franklin and The Impressions, this great God Almighty Everlasting, *et in terra pax hominibus*, and all them other good things, drew back his mighty arm—

"Watch your aim now, Lord."

And unloosed the giant thunderbolt. BOOM!

That was the end of Stagolee. You can't mess with the Lord.

Well, when the people found out Stagolee was dead, you ain't never heard such hollering and crying in all your life. The women were beside themselves with grief, 'cause Stagolee was nothing but a sweet man.

Come the day of the funeral, and Stagolee was laid out in a $10,000 casket. Had on a silk mohair suit and his Stetson hat was in his hand. In his right coat pocket was a brand new deck of cards. In his left coat pocket was a brand new .44 with some extra rounds of ammunition and a can of Mace. And by his side was his guitar. Folks came from all over the country to Stack's funeral, and all of 'em put little notes in Stagolee's other pockets, which were messages they wanted Stagolee to give to their kinfolk when he got to Hell.

The funeral lasted for three days and three nights. All the guitar pickers and blues singers had to come sing one last song for Stagolee. All the backsliders had to come backslide one more time for Stagolee. All the gamblers had to come touch Stack's casket for a little taste of good luck. And all the women had to come shed a tear as they looked at him for the last time. Those that had known him were crying about what they weren't going to have any more. And those that hadn't known him were crying over what they had missed. Even the little bitty ones was shedding tears.

After all the singing and crying and shouting was over, they took Stagolee on out and buried him. They didn't bury him in the cemetery. Uh-uh. Stagolee had to have a cemetery all his own. They dug his grave with a silver spade and lowered him down with a golden chain. And they went on back to their homes, not quite ready to believe that Stack was dead and gone.

But you know, it's mighty hard to keep a good man down, and, long about the third day, Stagolee decided to get on up out of the grave and go check out Heaven. Stack just couldn't see himself waiting for Judgment Day. The thought of that white man blowing the trumpet on Judgment Day made him sick to his stomach, and Stagolee figured he was supposed to have his own Judgment Day, anyhow.

He started on off for Heaven. Of course it took him a long time to get there, 'cause he had to stop on all the clouds and teach the little angels how to play Pitty-Pat and Coon-Can and all like that, but, eventually, he got near to Heaven. Now as he got close, he started hearing all this harp music and hymn singing. Stagolee couldn't believe his ears. He listened some more, and then he shrugged his shoulders. "I'm approaching Heaven from the wrong side. This can't be the black part of Heaven, not with all that hymn singing and harp music I hear."

So Stack headed on around to the other side of Heaven, and when he got there, it was stone deserted. I mean, wasn't nobody there. Streets was as empty as the President's mind. So Stack cut on back around to the other side of Heaven. When he got there, St. Peter was playing bridge with Abraham, Jonah, and Mrs. God. When they looked up and saw who it was, though, they split, leaving St. Peter there by himself.

"You ain't getting in here!" St. Peter yelled.

"Don't want to, either. Hey, man. Where all the colored folks at?"

"We had to send 'em all to Hell. We used to have quite a few, but they got to rocking the church service, you know. Just couldn't even sing a hymn without it coming out and sounding like the blues. So we had to get rid of 'em. We got a few nice colored folks left. And they nice, respectable people."

Stagolee laughed. "Hey, man. You messed up."

"Huh?"

"Yeah, man. This ain't Heaven. This is Hell. Bye."

And Stagolee took off straight for Hell. He

was about 2,000 miles away, and he could smell the barbecue cooking and hear the jukeboxes playing, and he started running. He got there, and there was a big BLACK POWER sign on the gate. He rung on the bell, and the dude who come to answer it recognized him immediately. "Hey, everybody! Stagolee's here!"

And the folks came running from everywhere to greet him.

"Hey, baby!"

"What's going down!"

"What took you so long to get here?"

Stagolee walked in, and the brothers and sisters had put down wall-to-wall carpeting, indirect lighting, and, best of all, they'd installed air-conditioning. Stagolee walked around, checking it all out. "Yeah. Y'all got it together. Got it uptight!"

After he'd finished checking it out, he asked, "Any white folks down here?"

"Just the hip ones, and ain't too many of them. But they all right. They know where it's at."

"Solid." Stagolee noticed an old man sitting over in a corner with his hands over his ears. "What's his problem?"

"Aw, that's the Devil. He just can't get himself together. He ain't learned how to deal with niggers yet."

Stagolee walked over to him. "Hey, man. Get your pitchfork, and let's have some fun. I got my .44. C'mon. Let's go one round."

The Devil just looked at Stagolee real sad-like, but didn't say a word.

Stagolee took the pitchfork and laid it on the shelf. "Well, that's hip. I didn't want no stuff out of you nohow. I'm gon' rule Hell by myself!"

And that's just what he did, too.

People

The Old Man
Who Wouldn't Take Advice

Once there was an old man who owned a big farm in Louisiana. He was fairly rich and didn't have to worry in his old age. His sons took care of the farm and managed all the business. All he had to do was sit on the porch and enjoy his old age.

He couldn't totally enjoy himself, though, because his wife had died, and he was lonely. And you know an old man. He don't want nothing he can handle. Uh-uh. He got to find the youngest, fastest woman that'll have him, and this old man wasn't too much different. Every Saturday, he'd go into town and sit around the courthouse and just watch the girls go by. And when he saw one that he liked, he was after her. For an old man, he could get around well, too. So it wasn't any problem for him to chase the young girls all over town.

One day, he met a girl he thought was the one. She was young, good-looking, knew how to take care of a house, and, after he told her how much money he had, she fell in love with him. Soon they were married.

Well, this wasn't one of those old men who just wanted a young girl for show. No, indeed! Not this old man! He hoped he'd never get that old. On their wedding night, he went to his young bride in eager anticipation, and he cried when he found out that he'd lost his powers. In all of his years, that had never happened, and he'd never had a reason to think that it would. But it had, and his young wife let him know in no uncertain terms what she was going to do if he didn't do something.

The next morning, he went into town to see the doctor. Doctor examined him and found him to be in good shape. "Jake! You're an old man

with a young man's dreams. That's your problem. And there ain't a thing a doctor can do." Ol' Jake couldn't accept that. And he went to another doctor who said much the same thing. He spent weeks going to doctors all over the state, and they all told him that medicine wouldn't do him a bit of good.

He went to see a root doctor. Now you know, down there in Louisiana they got the best root doctors in the country. They got some root doctors know just what remedy will cure everything from ugliness to death. These modern doctors don't know a thing with all their pills. You find you a good root doctor, and you don't have to worry about nothing except taxes, 'cause you'll have death licked. So Jake went to a root doctor, and she fixed him up a concoction and told him not to drink it until the third night of the full moon. Well, that was almost two weeks away, and Jake couldn't wait that long. He went home and drank it that night.

What'd he do that for? He should've done what the root doctor said and waited. Uh-uh. He couldn't wait. He drank that concoction, and, the second the last drop slid down his throat, he went stone blind. Jake couldn't have seen the sun if it had been sitting on his nose. Stone blind!

Well, Jake was really upset now, and he went back to the root doctor to see if she could give him another concoction to get his eyes back. She told him that if he'd followed her directions, he wouldn't have lost his sight, and she wouldn't have anything more to do with him.

Jake wanted to lay down and die. He'd lost his powers, and now he couldn't see. There he was, sitting on the front porch, as blind as white folks to racism. So he just sat and waited for Death to come.

One morning he was sitting on the porch when a pigeon flew in his lap.

"Please, old man. Please. Hide me in your coat. A hawk's after me, and if you don't hide me, he'll eat me. If you hide me, I'll see that you get your eyesight back."

Ol' Jake shoved the pigeon under his coat just as the hawk landed on the edge of the porch.

"Please, old man," said the hawk. "I'm hungry. Hungry as I can be, and that pigeon is the first thing I've seen to eat in two days. If you let the pigeon go, I'll see to it that you get your powers back."

Now you have to understand that this was down in Louisiana, and that's the one state that has more voodoo and conjuring than practically any place in the world. So ol' Jake wasn't surprised that the birds could talk or that they could promise to give him his eyesight and his powers back. He didn't know what to do, though. If he had his eyes, at least, he could see his wife and land. But what he could do if he had his powers back!

"Make up your mind," said the hawk. "I'm about to die from starvation."

Jake called his wife and explained the situation to her. "Well, if you don't know, don't ask me. I guess you want your eyes back. Humph! You better give that pigeon to that hawk and in a hurry. What I care if you see?" And she cussed the old man out again.

Well, he was really confused now, because he wanted to make her happy, but he missed being able to see everything that went on. So he didn't do anything. After a while, one of his old buddies came by and Jake told him all about it.

"Now I tell you, Jake. I figure it's always better to see. That way you can see if something's creeping up on you, and you can see if that young wife you got is creeping out on you. If you got your powers back, that don't mean she still wouldn't sneak out now and then. At least if you had your eyes back, you could keep an eye on her."

The Old Man Who Wouldn't Take Advice

Jake didn't know what to do. He weighed both of their arguments, and both made a lot of sense. But he wasn't totally satisfied with either one. And if he didn't do what his wife told him to do, she would leave him. But if he didn't do what his buddy told him to do, he'd lose a lifelong friend. Whichever way he went, he was going to lose. So he just didn't do anything.

The hawk was still sitting on the edge of the porch, and the pigeon was quivering underneath his shirt. Jake put his hand on the pigeon to try and calm it when he chuckled to himself.

He called one of his grandchildren and whispered in his ear. Then he turned to the hawk. "All right, hawk. You win. But you can't have the pigeon now. Come back in an hour."

"Can't you make it half an hour?"

"Naw. An hour, and the pigeon is yours."

The hawk flew away, and, the minute it was out of sight, Jake said to the pigeon, "You promised me my eyes back, didn't you?"

"Yes, but you're going to give me to the hawk."

"No, I'm not. Not if you keep your promise."

"If you let me go, you'll get your eyes back."

Well, about forty-five minutes later, Jake's

grandson came on the porch and gave him a covered basket. Jake reached in the basket and pulled out a pigeon. He opened his shirt and the pigeon flew out, and, sure enough, Jake's eyes came back in time to see the pigeon flying away. He wanted to stand up and shout, but he didn't have time. The hawk would be coming back at any minute.

Sure enough. He had barely put the other pigeon in his shirt when the hawk landed on the edge of the porch.

"You promised to give me my powers back," he said to the hawk.

"You got 'em if I get the pigeon."

Jake unbuttoned his shirt, and the pigeon flew out, and the hawk pounced on him and took him to the far reaches of the sky. And Jake felt his powers return.

Thus Jake got everything he wanted, because he made up his own mind and didn't let his wife or his friend do it for him.

People Who Could Fly

It happened long, long ago, when black people were taken from their homes in Africa and forced to come here to work as slaves. They were put onto ships, and many died during the long voyage across the Atlantic Ocean. Those that survived stepped off the boats into a land they had never seen, a land they never knew existed, and they were put into the fields to work.

Many refused, and they were killed. Others

would work, but when the white man's whip lashed their backs to make them work harder, they would turn and fight. And some of them killed the white men with the whips. Others were killed by the white men. Some would run away and try to go back home, back to Africa where there were no white people, where they worked their own land for the good of each other, not for the good of white men. Some of those who tried to go back to Africa would walk until they came to the ocean, and then they would walk into the water, and no one knows if they did walk to Africa through the water or if they drowned. It didn't matter. At least they were no longer slaves.

Now when the white man forced Africans onto the slave-ships, he did not know, nor did he care, if he took the village musicians, artists, or witch doctors. As long as they were black and looked strong, he wanted them—men, women, and children. Thus, he did not know that sometimes there would be a witch doctor among those he had captured. If he had known, and had also known that the witch doctor was the medium of the gods, he would have thought twice. But he did not care. These black men and black women were not people to him. He looked at them and counted each one as so much money for his pocket.

It was to a plantation in South Carolina that one boatload of Africans was brought. Among them was the son of a witch doctor who had not completed by many months studying the secrets of the gods from his father. This young man carried with him the secrets and powers of the generations of Africa.

One day, one hot day when the sun singed the very hair on the head, they were working in the fields. They had been in the fields since before the sun rose, and, as it made its journey to the highest part of the sky, the very air seemed to be on fire. A young woman, her body curved with the child that grew deep inside her, fainted.

Before her body struck the ground, the white man with the whip was riding toward her on his horse. He threw water in her face. "Get back to work, you lazy nigger! There ain't going to be no sitting down on the job as long as I'm here." He cracked the whip against her back and, screaming, she staggered to her feet.

All work had stopped as the Africans watched, saying nothing.

"If you niggers don't want a taste of the same, you'd better get to work!"

They lowered their heads and went back to work. The young witch doctor worked his way slowly toward the young mother-to-be, but before he could reach her, she collapsed again, and the white man with the whip was upon her, lashing her until her body was raised from the ground by the sheer violence of her sobs. The young witch doctor worked his way to her side and whispered something in her ear. She, in turn, whispered to the person beside her. He told the next person, and on around the field it went. They did it so quickly and quietly that the white man with the whip noticed nothing.

A few moments later, someone else in the field fainted, and, as the white man with the whip rode toward him, the young witch doctor shouted, "Now!" He uttered a strange word, and the person who had fainted rose from the ground, and moving his arms like wings, he flew into the sky and out of sight.

The man with the whip looked around at the Africans, but they only stared into the distance, tiny smiles softening their lips. "Who did that? Who was that who yelled out?" No one said anything. "Well, just let me get my hands on him."

Not too many minutes had passed before the young woman fainted once again. The man was almost upon her when the young witch doctor shouted, "Now!" and uttered a strange word.

She, too, rose from the ground and, waving her arms like wings, she flew into the distance and out of sight.

This time the man with the whip knew who was responsible, and as he pulled back his arm to lash the young witch doctor, the young man yelled, "Now! Now! Everyone!" He uttered the strange word, and all of the Africans dropped their hoes, stretched out their arms, and flew away, back to their home, back to Africa.

That was long ago, and no one now remembers what word it was that the young witch doctor knew that could make people fly. But who knows? Maybe one morning someone will awake with a strange word on his tongue and, uttering it, we will all stretch out our arms and take to the air, leaving these blood-drenched fields of our misery behind.

Keep on Stepping

You know, white folks are something else. Always been like they are now. Just don't want to let a nigger be a man. Somehow they figure if you become a man, they ain't one no longer.

Back during slavery time, there was a black man by the name of Dave. He was slaving on a plantation somewhere in Tennessee. One day he was out working in the field, and he saw ol' massa and ol' missy's two children out in a boat, screaming. They'd lost the oars, and the boat was out of control, spinning around, and they were about to be thrown into the water.

Now if Dave had been a field nigger like High John, he would've swum out there and tipped the boat over. Dave wasn't like that. He'd probably been working in the sun too long and couldn't think straight. Anyway, he ran to the big house and told massa and missy.

Ol' missy hollered out, "Somebody save my children! I ain't never gon' have no more, and them the only two I got."

So Dave ran down to the river, jumped in, and saved the two children. Well, ol' massa and missy was mighty happy, and massa told Dave, "Well, nigger, if you make a good crop this year and fill up the barn and work 'till the crops are laid by next year, I'll give you your freedom."

That's what I mean about white folks. He couldn't give Dave his freedom just because he'd saved the children. Uh-uh. Dave had to save the children, plus do all the plowing and planting and hoeing the next year; then, if he did all that, he'd get his freedom. Dave was free all the time. Just didn't know how to enforce it.

Anyway, Dave worked like a champ to make a good crop that year. He made such a good crop that it not only filled the barn, but half the house, too. So, after the crops were laid by the next summer, massa called Dave in the house.

"Well, Dave. I'm a man of my word. You're a free nigger today. I sho' hate to get rid of a good nigger like you, but I promised."

So he gave Dave one of his old suits of clothes and a few other things. The children were crying, and ol' missy was crying, and ol' massa was kinda sniffing himself. But Dave tied the clothes in a bundle and put 'em on the end of a stick, and took off down the road, walking real slow.

Ol' massa called out after him. "Dave! The children love you."

"Yassuh," Dave called back.

"Dave, I love you."

"Yassuh."

"And missy, she like you."

"Yassuh."

"But remember, Dave. You still a nigger."

As long as Dave was in sight, massa was standing there on the porch, hollering, "Dave! The children love you. I love you, and missy, she like you. But, remember, Dave! You still a nigger!"

Dave would holler back, "Yassuh," but he kept right on stepping until he got to Canada. Even though massa had let Dave's body go free, he still

wanted to keep him a slave by yelling, "Remember, you still a nigger."

You ain't free long as you let somebody else tell you who you are. We got black people today walking around in slavery 'cause they let white folks tell 'em who they are. But you be like Dave. Just keep on stepping, children, when you know you're right. Don't matter what they yell after you. Just keep on stepping.

All the stories in this book, except for one, can be found in other collections of folktales as told by other story tellers. Those versions, as well as many more good stories, appear in the books mentioned below.

"How God Made the Butterflies" and "How the Snake Got His Rattles" can both be found in Zora Neale Hurston's fine book *Mules and Men* (Philadelphia: J. B. Lippincott, 1939). Unfortunately, this book is out of print. It is one of the few books that set black folktales in their social environment and show their social and political functions.

"Why Apes Look Like People" exists in a shorter version in *Nigerian Folk Tales*, told to and edited by Barbara K. and Warren S. Walker (New Brunswick: Rutgers University Press, 1961).

"Why Men Have to Work" is an African tale traditionally known as "Why the Sky Is Far Away." A version under that title appears in *The Origin of Life and Death: African Creation Myths*, edited by Ulli Beier (London: Heinemann, 1966).

"The Girl With the Large Eyes" can be found in a collection by Bakare Gbadamosi and Ulli Beier, *Not Even God Is Ripe Enough: Yoruba Stories* (London: Heinemann, 1968) under the title "Large Eyes Produce Many Tears."

"The Son of Kim-ana-u-eze and the Daughter of the Sun and the Moon" is an Ambundu tale. There is a version of it in *African Myths and Tales*, edited by Susan Feldman (New York: Dell, 1963).

"Jack and the Devil's Daughter" is a well-known black folktale existing in many versions. Zora Neale Hurston's *Mules and Men* (mentioned above) includes it, as does *American Negro Folktales*, edited by Richard M. Dorson (New York: Fawcett Premier, 1957).

The folk hero High John the Conqueror is also known as

John, Jack, and Trickster John. There are many stories involving John and the white man, and the "High John the Conqueror" story I have told uses the outline of two separate ones. Stories about John can be found in practically any collection of Afro-American tales.

"Stagolee" is a song that exists in many versions. Perhaps the most complete printed one is in the Alan Lomax book *Folk Songs of North America* (Garden City: Doubleday, 1960). The story of Stagolee that I tell uses the song as its base and evolves from my own version, which I recorded on my first Vanguard album.

"The Old Man Who Wouldn't Take Advice" can be found in the Gbadamosi and Beier book mentioned above, under the title "A Wise Man Solves His Own Problems."

"People Who Could Fly" appears in the Langston Hughes and Arna Bontemps collection, *The Book of Negro Folklore* (New York: Dodd, Mead & Co., 1958). It was once common to hear this story throughout the coastal regions of South Carolina and Georgia. Sources for the Federal Writer's Project book *Drums and Shadows* refer to it constantly as if it were fact. It may be.

"Keep on Stepping" does exist in other printed versions, but I haven't been able to locate any, and I don't remember where I got it from.

Other Grove Press Paperbacks

☐ ALLEN, DONALD M., ed. *The New American Poetry.* E237/$5.95
☐ ARSAN, EMMANUELLE, *Emmanuelle.* B361/$1.95
                    —*Emmanuelle II.* B383/$1.95

☐ BECKETT, SAMUEL, *Three Novels. Molloy; Malone Dies; The Unnamable.*
                    B78/$3.95
                    —*Endgame.* E96/$1.95
                    —*Waiting for Godot.* E33/$1.95

☐ BERNE, ERIC, M.D. *Games People Play.* B186/$1.95
                    —*A Layman's Guide to Psychiatry and Psychoanalysis.*
                    B380/$1.95
☐ BRAUTIGAN, RICHARD. *A Confederate General from Big Sur.* B283/$1.95
☐ BRECHT, BERTOLT. *Galileo.* B120/$1.95
                    —*Mother Courage and Her Children.* B108/$1.95
☐ BURROUGHS, WILLIAM S. *Naked Lunch.* B115/$1.95
☐ CUMMINGS, E. E. *100 Selected Poems.* E190/$1.95
☐ FANON, FRANTZ. *The Wretched of the Earth.* B342/$1.95
☐ GENET, JEAN. *The Balcony.* E130/$2.95
☐ IONESCO, EUGENE, *Four Plays. The Bald Soprano; The Lesson; The Chairs;*
                    Jack, or The Submission. E101/$2.95
☐ KEROUAC, JACK. *The Subterraneans.* B300/$1.50
☐ LAWRENCE, D. H. *Lady Chatterley's Lover.* B9/$1.95
☐ MALCOLM X. *Autobiography of Malcolm X.* B146/$1.95
☐ MILLER, HENRY. *Tropic of Cancer.* B10/$1.95
                    —*Tropic of Capricorn.* B59/$1.95
☐ PINTER, HAROLD. *The Homecoming.* E411/$1.95
☐ REAGE, PAULINE. *Story of O.* B396/$1.95
☐ SCHUTZ, WILLIAM C. *Joy.* B323/$1.95
☐ SNOW, EDGAR. *Red Star Over China.* E618/$4.95
☐ STOPPARD, TOM. *Rosencrantz & Guildenstern Are Dead.* B319/$1.95
                    —*Travesties.* E661/$1.95
☐ SUZUKI, D. T. *Introduction to Zen Buddhism.* B341/$1.95
☐ TRUFFAUT, FRANCOIS. *The Story of Adele H.* B395/$2.45

At your bookstore, or order below.

Grove Press Inc., 196 West Houston St., New York, N.Y. 10014.

Please mail me the books checked above. I am enclosing $_____.
(No COD. Add 35¢ per book for postage and handling.)

Name _____

Address_____

City_____State_____Zip_____